THE GUARDIAN'S NECKLACE

by
Donald Brown

Special Thanks

I would like to thank Junyi (Shelly) Xiao from Jersey School for Girls for her cover illustrations, and Lauren Etchells, another Jersey writer, for her editorial assistance.

CHAPTER ONE

J osh woke to the smell of canvas and wood smoke and a faint sense of unease. He rubbed his eyes and tried to focus. Where was he? Northwoods Island, camped between the pine woods and the beach.

He reached over and undid the tent flap , catching a sudden blast of cold morning air. The sweet smell of pine wood drifted on the breeze. This was what they had come for! His stepdad had led them on a detour through the woods and found this deserted spot on the northern tip of the island. He and Megs had planned to get up early and explore those woods. He groped around for his watch. Six o'clock. He struggled out of his sleeping bag, pulled back the tent flap and peered through the hanging mist.

Getting up early was Megs' idea. Sometimes, you wouldn't think it, but she was only twelve years old, nearly two years younger than himself. Getting up early was an adventure at that age. He expected to see her peering out of her tent, ready to dash across and wake him.

He stepped outside and stood barefoot on the damp grass and looked around him. He blinked and stared. But he saw no tent and no Megs.

In the place where her tent should have been, he saw a flattened patch of grass and odd strips of canvas attached to bent skewers; beyond that, a white bundle of canvas tossed in a crumpled heap at the edge of the woods.

He threw a coat over his pyjamas and looked around him, shivering in the breeze. There could have been a gale in the night. He thought he'd heard something; more like the sound of animals scampering across the campsite. Or was that part of his dream? He scanned the edge of the woods, hoping to see Megs sitting on her rucksack waiting for him to help her with the tent.

His eyes returned to that white bundle of canvas tossing in the breeze. Somehow it didn't look right. There wasn't enough of it. He raced across the grass to investigate. He pulled the tent away from the trees and ran his hands along the sides of the canvas. It looked as if someone had sliced it away from the groundsheet. Pirates had done this! A year ago, he'd have said colonists. But he hadn't seen any colonists on this strange island. It must have been his own people who'd done this. No sign of the groundsheet! No sleeping bag either! They must have seized the sheet by its four corners and carried Megs off with them, sleeping bag and all, into the woods.

But why Megs? He was the one with the stone. That's what they wanted, of course; not that it would be of any use to them! He raced back to his tent and threw on his clothes, thoughts pounding through his head. Why hadn't they seized him instead? He struggled into his trousers. Socks. Where were his socks? Perhaps they'd tried? Forget about socks. Shoes! Where were his shoes? But he always kept his stone hidden. Of course! That's why they'd gone for Megs. They wanted him to give up his stone to get her free. So they'd contact him soon and tell him where to meet. He stared into the dark woods. They couldn't be far away. Quickly! Finding them first would give him a slight edge. He grabbed his stone; he'd hide it along the way.

His parents had pitched their tent at the edge of the cliff. He ran in, unzipped the sleeping compartment and shouted, "Dad. Wake up!"

His stepdad's startled face rose a few inches from the pillow of his sleeping-bag. He rubbed his eyes and looked around him, passing a hand through his mop of straw hair. "Ham and handlebars," he said, in a faraway voice. "Oh, it's you Josh. You're up early. Off on an expedition somewhere? Good idea." His voice tailed away as his head touched the pillow again.

"Wake up, Dad. This is serious. They've taken Megs. No time to explain!"

This time his stepdad shot up as if he'd been jabbed in the ribs. "Hey, Josh! Wait!"

Josh hardly heard him as he raced away. His stepdad could call the emergency services or whatever. He couldn't wait for that. Megs needed his help now!

Beyond Meg's tent lay a sandy path leading deep into the woods. He sprinted through the pine trees, placed at regular intervals on either side of the path, seeing the way ahead for a hundred yards or so in the flickering light. Then the undergrowth grew denser, blocking his view. He had to slow up. The enemy could be waiting behind any bush or tree.

He stopped at a fork in the path. His instinct told him to take the narrower path on the right which wound out of sight through the undergrowth. He thought of using his stone to know for sure. But there wasn't time. Besides, he knew they'd have taken the wider path on his left; if he took this other path, he had a chance of creeping up on them unseen. He hurried down it, heart beating fast like a hunter afraid of its prey. She couldn't be far away. He stopped for a moment, thinking he heard a human noise; a cough or a muttered word. Then he saw a lighter patch ahead, a space in the trees. This looked like a likely place. He dived into a clump of bushes and edged his way forwards.

Thoughts thumped through his mind again. He had to play for time until help arrived. He had to hide his stone – but keep it in reach. Use it to bargain with but never give it up – something told him those people would kill them both if they got what they came for. The brambles pricked his arms and he could hardly see. Noiselessly, he brushed some branches aside to get a better view.

A large, oblong object stood in the open space. He slowly pushed his way upwards into a standing position and peered down at it through the leaves. He gulped when he realised what they'd done.

Her face stared upwards like a hooked fish from the open end of a shallow, wooden chest. A long steel blade like a paper cutter hung poised across her neck. He clenched the stone in his pocket. What kind of people would do that to a kid like Megs? He braced himself to make a dash from his hiding place and run to her side, but he heard light footsteps approaching down the path. He dropped silently to the ground again and flattened himself among the leaves, struggling to control his breathing.

He saw the figure of a woman out for a walk. He began to breathe normally again. Maybe she could help him? Between them, they could get Megs free – or he could do it himself while the woman went back for help. She'd be here in a minute. He'd ask her. He saw her clearly now; a tall, athletic figure in black jeans and a frilly, white shirt. She had short, fair hair and black, pearl earrings…She…

Just then the woman turned and stared directly at the place where he was hiding. He caught a sudden glimpse of those catlike eyes. She couldn't see him, could she? He gripped the stone in his pocket and stood motionless behind the thin screen of leaves. Those eyes seemed fixed on him; empty, inquisitive, intent on mischief. A casual visitor out for a walk? No chance! This was Catharine Cattermole! The Cat Lady!

Her eyes switched away from him and she was a woman again. She looked out of place in these woods; like a nurse in uniform doing her rounds. He watched, mesmerised, as she settled on the coffin lid.

"Are you comfy in this little bed I've made for you, darling?" she asked in a sweet soft voice, peering down at Megs.

He rose noiselessly to his feet to get a better view. He saw her reach down a hand to finger Megs' neck. She extracted a tissue from her pocket.

"Poor child," she murmured. "You've cut yourself. Let me wipe away the blood for you."

He heard a defiant croak. "Don't touch me!"

The lady's smile flashed a warning. "Let me have a good look at you." He saw Megs flinch, as those teasing eyes inspected her face.

"Poor Megs! How can I make you more comfortable until your boyfriend arrives?"

"I haven't got a boyfriend. Let me go!"

Josh's muscles tightened again as he watched Megs' frightened face, staring upwards like a patient in a dentist's chair, tensing herself against any sudden movement.

"It won't be long now. He'll soon be here. Would you like me to take this metal thing away from your neck?"

"Just do it!"

"Of course, dear!"

Suddenly, she leaned over and touched something on the side of the coffin. He tensed his fists.

"Ow, my throat!"

He choked back the urge to cry out.

Her face was close to Megs' now. Josh caught the quick smile and the tinkling laugh. "Silly me! I touched the wrong button. But it's so tempting, isn't it?" She dabbed Megs' brow and touched another button which made the blade fly upwards an inch. "Don't worry. I'm not going to harm you. You can move your head now. You're free! Well, almost. You see, it's the boy they want. He's got my master's stone and my master needs it."

He heard the relief in Meg's voice as she found she could turn her neck. "The stone belongs to Josh!" she cried. It's the

Guardian's stone!"

The Cat Lady stared at her. "You'd think so, wouldn't you? My master thinks it's his!"

"The stone of truth?" Megs snorted. He could see she was past caring now. "What would any friend of yours want with the truth?"

Josh's heart swelled with pride for Megs and her bravery. He held his breath, fearing that some terrible punishment would follow. Instead, he noticed a glint of satisfaction in the Cat Lady's eyes. She turned away as if she had other things on her mind. Then she was back again with a plan. "I see you're getting cross. I think it's time to call the boy. Maybe he can help us both."

Josh's hands rushed to his pockets. He had to silence that phone. Then he remembered with relief that he had forgotten to bring it with him. Would his dad go to the tent and pick it up? What would he say? And what kind of help would he summon up and when?

She sat upright and tapped out the numbers on her phone. She held it in her hand a long time. She turned to Megs. "Strange. He must be a heavy sleeper, your boyfriend. Oh, hello. That's Mr Flagsmith, isn't it? … That's right. Catharine Cattermole…Yes, the PE teacher at your school. A long time ago. How time flies when you're busy!... No, don't say anything. I'd like to speak to Josh if you don't mind. Well, really! There's no need to be offensive. I am sure we can work this out amicably. I've got a young lady here who's in a bit of a fix. Yes, Megs. She's under my protection. Listen!" The Cat Lady pointed a finger at Megs and poked it in her eye.

Megs shrieked. The sudden jolt caused her to raise her head and cut her neck again on the blade.

"You see? I told you not to say anything. Megs needs your help straightaway. So, tell Josh to come quickly and he may be able to save her. It's very easy. I can see your tents over there near the shore. Just tell him to follow the path behind you into the woods. When he gets to the fork, he's to turn left. He will see us just a little further on, relaxing in a little glade. At least, I'm relaxing. I don't know about Megs. No! Don't try to follow him or you'll put both their lives in danger. We don't want that, do we? Sorry, I can't hear you… I'll take that as a no…. Oh! And – silly me! – I almost forgot. Tell him to bring his stone. That's all we require of him. I'm sure you'll be able to make him see sense."

The Cat Lady disappeared in the direction of the tents. She probably aimed to lie in wait for him at the edge of the glade.

Josh hesitated. He looked through the bushes in the direction where the Cat Lady had gone. He felt a wrench in his stomach as he parted with his stone, hiding it in the mud beneath his feet. He covered it with leaves and raced into the open to kneel beside the coffin.

"Megs," he whispered. "Sh! Stay still! No! Megs, don't move or you'll hurt yourself."

He saw her pale, trapped face tremble with relief.

He followed with his eyes the intricate wiring of the buttons attached to the side of the coffin. A sticker with a lopsided smiley face caught his eye for a second. He pressed the lower button. The steel blade sprang back a little.

"Careful, Josh!"

"Don't worry, Megs. I'll be careful. I'll have you free in seconds."

"She's coming back!"

"Only a second." He pressed the lower button one more time, but nothing happened.

"Just do it!" she screamed. Her limbs had gone rigid with desperation.

This time he pressed harder. The guillotine gave a little judder and then a click. Suddenly he saw the blade rise a full six inches from her neck.

"I'm free! I'm free!" cried Megs, bursting into tears. "I can move my head. I'm free!"

"Stay still, Megs! Freeze! It's not over yet." He reviewed his handiwork. "Look Megs, this is the best I can do. I am going to haul you out. Just keep your head away from that blade." Holding her by the shoulders, he used all his strength to extricate her frozen body from the coffin and drag her like a limp fish onto the ground. She hopped and stumbled around in joy, hugging him until he gasped aloud for breath.

"What about your stepdad?" she whispered.

"He knows!"

"Have you got the stone?"

"She's not getting it. Sh!"

"I knew you'd come! They told me they wanted your stone!"

"Weren't you scared?"

"Of course, I was scared, but I knew it wasn't for ever."

"How are you feeling now?"

Her eyes widened. "Wonderful! I feel wonderful!" she said.

"Sh!"

The sound of a cracking twig prompted him to look up. Maybe he should have kept his stone with him after all. A group of soldiers had materialised from nowhere and formed a circle around the coffin.

"Stay there! Don't move!" A tall pirate with a hooked nose and joyless eyes came and stood over him. He wore a ragged dark green pullover smelling of sweat and pipe tobacco. Josh looked beyond him at the other soldiers, sheathed daggers hanging from their belts, legs apart, chests puffed out, staring.

"So you're the pirate Guardian, the boy with the stone," said the man, staring at Josh with loathing. "Your father's an important man in these parts, I hear. I suppose that's how he fixed your selection. You're not the only pirate to be born with the 'gift' as they like to call it. Where I come from, we don't hold with Guardians. What can you do for us besides prophesy and preach peace?" He pointed to the scar running down the side of his right cheek. "A colonist did this to me. And he wasn't preaching peace, I can tell you."

A few of the soldiers nudged one another and laughed.

With Megs at his side, Josh felt brave. He kept his arm around her shoulders and stared at the opposition. They wore combat fatigues but they didn't look like soldiers. Why no guns? Two of them were old men. They shuffled their feet and turned away from his stare. There was one boy, probably not much older than himself, who hung his head and stared at his boots. If he'd got his stone, maybe he'd have the strength to get inside their heads. But he couldn't risk fetching it from its hiding place.

Just then, a fat balding man lit a cigarette. He had 'The Rebel Prince' printed on his shirt. Who was this 'Prince'? He must be a pirate; only pirates gave themselves names like that.

The men stiffened to attention. The Cat Lady had returned. She walked through them, swinging her hips, as if they didn't exist, with a gleam of command in her eyes. "Ah, Josh!" she said in a teasing voice. "The young Guardian! The boy with the gift! Mind you, your famous 'gift' is not much use in a tight situation like this."

Josh knew from the mischievous glitter in her eyes that she'd found his weak spot. If she could bring on a fit with her taunting, she'd get what she came for. "I thought you worked for the colonists," he said, loud enough for her followers to hear. "Killing pirates used to be your thing."

He knew as soon as he said it that words cut no ice with these pirates. One or two of them stared at the ground, but they'd made their decision, and nothing would budge them now. The Cat Lady herself just smiled. "Go on," she said. "Talk. What else can you do; froth at the mouth and have visions. Well, I suppose your stone would give you strength – but I see you're looking worried so maybe you haven't got it with you!"

She came close enough to smile at him. Then her eyes flickered away again as if she'd lost interest. She turned and waved a dramatic arm at the circle of soldiers. "I would like to introduce you to my friends. Of course, you will be glad to know that they are all pirates like yourself. Well, not quite like yourself, actually. They come from Windfree; the island of peace and freedom where my master rules."

Who was her master? He thought of that smiley face on the coffin. Just the sort of cynical logo that would appeal to Ronald Fleck! But did he live in Windfree? He wasn't a pirate. Nor was the Cat Lady. Maybe that was the connection. He suppressed a shudder.

The Cat Lady was speaking to Megs now. She pointed to her soldiers. "There you are," she said, "'Peace and Freedom' – it's printed on their shirts."

Megs scowled. "Is that the kind of freedom you offered me in that coffin thing?" she asked.

"Freedom requires the occasional sacrifice," said the Cat Lady. You could tell she was getting bored with the conversation. "I am afraid my friends here are becoming impatient." She stared at Megs with her cruel, fathomless eyes. "Just ask your boyfriend to fetch me his stone, dear, and we'll all be happy."

"Some of us will be dead," said Megs, gripping Josh's arm.

"And I haven't got the stone," added Josh. "But I can tell you where to find it."

The Cat Lady's eyes sparkled with interest. "Better search him Walter, just in case. He may be telling the truth. In that case it won't be far away."

The pirate in the green pullover loomed over him. "Shirt," he said, extending a large, calloused hand.

Josh fumbled with his shirt.

"Shoes. You can give me your socks, too."

Josh stood in his bare feet.

Walter held out his hand again. "Trousers!" he commanded.

"Come off it!" cried Megs. "You can see he hasn't got it!"

Walter stared at Josh and reached for his long knife which he pointed at his midriff. "Do you want me to cut them off?" he asked.

Josh handed over his trousers and watched as Walter ripped open the pockets, letting his watch and a few coins spill onto the grass. He stood in his underpants, feeling as useless as a skinned frog.

"What about the girl?" asked Walter.

The Cat Lady shook her head. "No, the boy's the one, but he hasn't got it. We must help him remember where he put it." Josh could feel Megs tighten her hold on his arm. They both knew they were safe until the Cat Lady got what she came for. The pirates began to mutter among themselves and one or two reached for their knives.

The Cat Lady whispered something to Walter. She approached Josh again, all charm and sweetness. "I know how you feel, Josh. You want to put up a bit of a show in front of your girlfriend here. But what's the point? We'll get what we came for in the end."

Josh heard the distant sound of a helicopter landing in the woods. His heart beat faster at the prospect of rescue. The Cat Lady observed his reaction and smiled. "Reinforcements, no doubt; ours, not yours," she said. "So I am going to ask you again, nicely, one more time. Give me the stone."

Josh stared at her. Could she be bluffing? He had to keep a firm grip on the voice of reason. His stepdad would have called for help. It had to be on its way.

She had already lost interest in him. She had another plan on her mind. As she stood back and studied them, a smile formed at the corners of her mouth. "Now, are you ready, Megs? Yes, I'm sure Megs can help us."

"Don't touch her!" exclaimed Josh, standing between them.

Megs clung to his arm. "Don't bother to try and stop her! That's what she's after. She's a cat. That's her game."

The Cat Lady turned to her soldiers. "Walter Smearing," she called out. The man in the green pullover gave a knowing grin. "I hear you are handy with a knife. If Megs would favour us by standing against this tree."

Josh made a sudden lunge as he saw two pirates manhandling her and dragging her away. Two other pirates quickly grabbed him from behind and a sweaty arm lay across his windpipe, almost throttling him.

"You'll never get your wretched stone!" Megs cried as they shoved her against a pine tree and started lashing a rope around her arms and legs. "Don't try to stop them!" she shouted at Josh. "They're just looking for an excuse to beat you up."

Josh writhed, hot and breathless, in the hands of his captors. He watched as each pirate unsheathed his knife and laid it at Walter's feet. Then they stood back and waited for a word from the Cat Lady who stood in the centre of the glade.

"There's only one problem," said Josh, thinking fast on his feet. "I gave Megs the stone and only she knows where it's hidden."

The Cat Lady looked at him with amusement. "I don't believe you, Josh, but I'm willing to test your theory. Now remember, Walter, you are not supposed to kill her because she may have some information for us. So, let's start with the arms. And maybe, after the first throw, she will suddenly remember where she put the stone or Josh will remember for her."

Josh saw Megs struggling with the ropes that cut into her arms. Walter stood barely six feet away. He couldn't miss! "You're not much of a knife-thrower!" he taunted him. "Stand further back. Even I couldn't miss from that distance."

Walter didn't seem to hear him. Just then, Josh wriggled from the pirates' grasp and made a sudden lunge, trying to kick the knife from the pirate's hand. It was useless. The two pirates grabbed him again and dragged him to the edge of the circle. An elbow in his neck made him gasp for breath. Megs began to shake and sob. He went dizzy, watching her. Perhaps if he gave them the stone? Even in his desperation, he knew that wouldn't work. Once he told them where he'd hidden it, they were both as good as dead. "Don't worry, Megs!" he shouted. "Help's on its way. You'll see!"

The Cat Lady ignored him. "Are you ready, Walter?" she asked.

Walter wiped the blade on his jeans.

"You can throw when I give the word."

Walter nodded.

He saw it all in slow motion, like a scene pictured underwater. Everybody had gone still. Walter had raised his arm in readiness. The Cat Lady watched intently, all eyes upon her.

"Now!"

Josh jerked backwards. It was a while before he dared look up. Megs stood rigid, as if expecting the knife, but her chest heaved in quick pants and he couldn't see any blood. The pirates had gone very quiet. All eyes had switched to the knife-thrower. Walter Smearing's body had fallen forward like a useless sack, blood seeping from a hole in his head. The soldiers stood and stared at him, shocked and motionless. Even the Cat Lady looked confused.

Pistol fire rang out from the bushes on Josh's right.

"Get down! All of you! Get down!"

Nobody moved.

The bushes parted and two soldiers burst out of the wood; a giant of a man with a bald head and a moustache and a much shorter man who spoke with the calm certainty of being obeyed. "Down on the ground! Hands in front of you! Don't move!" he said in a matter-of-fact voice. He fired one shot in the air and said "That's better. Keep your heads down."

"That could have been you," he said to the Cat Lady. "No, don't smile. On the ground. Yes, you, too! Hands in front of you!"

He turned to Josh and said "Get down! Don't worry about Megs. Leave her! I'll attend to that."

He walked over and cut Megs free. Neither he nor his friend took much notice of the pirates, who lay prone on the ground. He strode over to Josh and pulled him to his feet. "Hi, Josh," he said, giving him a firm handshake, "I'm Captain Ketch. I'm in charge of this little operation. And that's Sergeant Jenkins. You're free to walk around now. These people aren't going anywhere. God knows why they didn't think to carry any firearms but I'm not complaining. You can make yourself useful by collecting up all their knives. You might want to recover your clothes too, before he bleeds all over them. Jenkins here will shoot anyone who dares to move. That one over there, maybe? He's reaching for his knife. Freeze! Withdraw your hand! That's right!"

Soon there was just one large sergeant with a pistol, sitting on a log and taking playful aim at the Cat Lady and the nine remaining pirates spread-eagled on the ground. He cracked a few jokes, but no one doubted that the bullets in his pistol were real.

"What will you do with the prisoners?" Megs asked the captain.

The captain faced her, hands on hips. "You're Megs, aren't you? A brave girl, I saw that."

Josh thought he saw most things.

"The Cat Lady's coming with us. In fact, you can handcuff her yourself, Megs. You'd like that, wouldn't you?"

Megs grinned.

"Miss Cattermole," the captain called out. "Stand over there by that tree! Never mind the smile. It's wasted on me, I'm afraid." He handed Megs the handcuffs. "Hands behind your back. There. Megs, you can do the rest. Tie her legs too. Loosely, mind. We're taking her with us."

"What about the rest of them?" asked Josh, struggling with the rope.

"The rest? Have you got all those knives? Good. Give them to me. I'll take care of them. After that, we'll just leave them. I doubt they're capable of doing us much harm. Very soon, the whole forest will be crawling with their army – if you can call it that – so we have no time to lose. We'll make a dash for the helicopter and get out of here before reinforcements arrive. How does that plan suit you, Megs?"

Josh knew what her answer would be.

"It sounds brilliant," she whispered, beaming.

CHAPTER TWO

At a shout from the captain – "Go! Go! Go!" – Josh grabbed Megs' hand, collected his stone from its hiding place, and pulled her stumbling through the trees to the helicopter, which had just landed in a swirling cloud of leaves and dust in a nearby clearing.

His mum hurried down the steps to help Megs up into the window seat beside her. Josh found a space beside his stepdad in the seat behind. Then the two soldiers arrived, pushing the Cat Lady ahead of them, and piled into the open floor space at the back. They handcuffed their captive to a metal bar at the side of the cabin where she sat shivering with head bowed throughout the journey.

Josh's mum cradled Megs in her arms, stroking her silky, black hair. "I thought I'd lost you for a moment," she murmured. "You're like a daughter to me, Megs. You know that." Slumped in his mother's arms, Megs looked like a kid of twelve again. That cruel coffin seemed a world away.

Josh spent most of the short return trip to Colony Island in silence. He didn't feel like talking above the roar of the rotor blades. He grabbed a glossy brochure from the sleeve in front of his seat. "Discover Northwoods, the undiscovered island beyond the mist!" He quickly returned it to its sleeve. He'd read that one. They all had! But so had everyone else! They'd landed in what looked like a building site. He wouldn't go back there in a hurry!

Behind him, he could see the Cat Lady's chest heaving rhythmically as she sobbed. Guilt didn't come into it. What was frightening her? The captain and Jenkins sat with their backs to her, cross-legged on their kitbags, playing cards. His stepdad stared out of the window, muttering to himself and shaking his head. Josh thought about Megs and the Cat Lady and that strange island which had taken them all by surprise. "How did you do it, Dad?" he asked. He wanted to add "and why couldn't you stop it happening?"

His stepdad had to shout to make himself heard above the roar of the blades. "The rescue, you mean? I'm not chief minister anymore, but I still have contacts in the secret service." He tossed his head back to indicate the captain and his sergeant. "They can get here in a few minutes from the heliport in the Last Resort…"

"You knew, didn't you?" Josh shouted. "You knew something was up!"

The noise of the rotor blades whirred to a halt. His stepdad lowered his voice in the sudden silence. "Yes, Josh," he said. "I realised the moment we arrived that Northwoods was a mistake. That's when I phoned the special forces." He ran a hand though his hair and looked at Josh with his intense, blue eyes. "I should have known before," he said in a small voice. "But I didn't. There it is."

His mum turned round in her seat. "How did we miss all this?" she asked. "I mean, Northwoods is on our doorstep. We should have realised that something strange was happening on that island!"

His stepdad's voice went up an octave – a sign that he was on the defensive. "I don't think we missed anything, dear," he said. "Don't forget that nobody had heard of the island until a year ago. Everything to the west of our little island was supposed to be beyond the edge of the world, remember?"

"I wish it still was!" Megs piped up from the seat in front.

Josh's mum gave Megs' shoulders a squeeze and whispered to her husband, "I think we'd better stop this conversation for the moment. We still have to decide what to do with Miss Cattermole."

"I could make a nice bed for her," muttered Megs, "but it might not be very comfortable."

Josh's mum laughed and stood up with her arm round Megs' shoulders. She waited beside the pilot for the steps to descend. Josh's stepdad tapped him on the shoulder. "You go ahead with your mum," he said. "I'll join you in a moment."

Josh left him talking to the captain and followed his mum across the tarmac to the empty aero club café.

He sat opposite his mum at a bare, metal table in a vast empty hall. She still had an arm round Megs, and smiled, but neither of them spoke. She started drumming her fingers on the table and looking at her watch. Megs opened her eyes and murmured in her ear, "He saved my life, you know."

His mum stroked her hair and nodded. "Sh! Megs," she whispered. "I know he did. I'm very proud of him."

Josh looked away, his stomach churning. His mum had no idea what the Cat Lady had put Megs through.

His stepdad burst through the swing doors and headed towards them with long, lanky strides.

"Have you ordered a taxi, dear?" asked his mum. "I'm due at the hospital in an hour. We're short-staffed; they need me."

His stepdad rubbed his eyes and stared into space.

"A taxi, dear," his mum reminded him.

"Oh yes. It's on its way."

Josh turned to him, wide awake and insistent. "Dad, do you know what the Cat Lady did to Megs back there?"

"I don't want to talk about it," said Megs, opening her eyes and looking around her for the first time.

"Hush dear, I know," said his mum.

Megs stood up and stretched her arms. Josh saw a glint of the old mischief returning to those dark eyes.

"Where are you going?" asked his mum.

"I'm feeling better now. I thought I'd have a word with the Cat Lady. She's still outside with the captain, isn't she? I just want to give her something."

"She has such a sweet nature, that girl," his mum whispered to her husband as Megs hurried out of the door.

His stepdad nodded absentmindedly.

Josh stared out of the window and tried not to smile. He could see Megs outside on the tarmac talking to the captain and Jenkins. The Cat Lady sat on a crate between them, with her head bowed, and her arms behind her back, handcuffed.

His mum started drumming on the table again with her long, slender fingers. "I hope she comes back soon," she said. "The taxi will be here shortly."

Just then they heard a shriek from outside on the tarmac.

"What was that noise?" asked his mum. "It sounded like Miss Cattermole."

Megs came running in, tucked her shirt into her jeans and took her place at the table with a secretive smile.

"What was all that about?" asked his mum.

"That? Oh, nothing," said Megs. "I just poked her in the eye."

"Well, really. Was that what you wanted to give her…?"

"Yes, I wanted her to know what it felt like."

"But didn't the captain try to stop you?"

"He didn't know what I was going to do."

His mum puckered her lips as if she didn't know whether to laugh or be angry. "There's more to you than meets the eye, Megs," she said, with a shake of her head.

Megs grinned. "Only my finger," she said. "That met her eye, all right."

His mum shook her head. Josh knew how she felt. Nothing she said would have made any difference when Megs was in this mood. Her toughness amazed him. It was he that couldn't get Northwoods out of his mind. So many questions whirled around in his brain that he didn't know where to start. He turned to his stepdad who'd hardly said anything since they'd arrived.

He fingered the stone in his pocket. "I just don't get it, Dad," he said.

"Get what, Josh?"

His parents exchanged glances.

"My stone," he said. "Why are people so interested in it all of a sudden?"

His mum frowned. "What do you mean, Josh?" she asked.

"You must have noticed it, mum! The moment we arrived on Northwoods, that's all everyone asked about."

His mum leaned back and laughed. "You're famous, Josh! You're the pirate Guardian. You dispersed the mist, remember? Without you, Northwoods wouldn't even feature on the map."

Josh stole a glance at his stepdad who coughed and looked away. Orthodox pirates like his mum believed that the great pirate Guardian, Matilda, had placed the mist like a solid wall across the westernmost tip of Colony Island to protect people from the lethal, red 'forget me flower' that lay beyond it. His stepdad still insisted – despite the evidence – that the mist was a freak of nature which simply came and went.

His mum smiled at him. "What are you really worried about, Josh?" she asked.

"Is it true, what that pirate said, that lots of pirates have the 'gift' and that I was only selected as Guardian because my dad's an important person?"

"What pirate said that, Josh?"

"Never mind. One of the pirates working for the Cat Lady, the one that got killed."

"That's nonsense, Josh. Your kind of epilepsy – the kind that enables you to have visions – is incredibly rare in the western isles. The moment you were born, you were marked out as special."

"Well, I knew about my epilepsy and being Guardian and stuff, but I didn't know I was special, not until two years ago when Reginald Machin started rounding up pirates and putting them in prison."

"You weren't needed before then, dear. But look how you managed! That's what your stone's for. It transforms your weakness into an incredible strength. No wonder all those people were curious about you."

Josh shook his head. "It's different this time, Mum!" he said. "It's about my stone. And I wouldn't just call it curious. Some of those islanders seemed to know that someone wants it."

"What kind of people, Josh?"

"Well, pirates, obviously. Most of the people on Northwoods seemed to be pirates like ourselves. But they were different somehow; not as friendly as they used to be."

"Yes, I noticed that. What do you think is their link with Miss Cattermole?"

Josh remembered those soldiers in the glade. "The Rebel Prince," he said.

His stepdad sat up. "Say that again, Josh," he said.

"The Rebel Prince. Those soldiers working for the Cat Lady – that's what was printed on their shirts."

His stepdad took a quick look round the hall. He lowered his voice. "That's what I was afraid of," he said. "There's a lot of poverty and unrest out there, especially among those pirates that suffered under Reggie Machin. If this man's calling himself the Rebel Prince, it sounds as if he wants to stir up trouble against the colonists like his famous ancestor."

His mum nodded. "The Guardian's necklace," she said. "If he's claiming to be descended from Rupert the Rebel, that must be what he's after."

Josh shifted uneasily in his seat. He could see from the serious expression on his parents' faces that something was troubling them, but he couldn't get a handle on it.

"You know about the necklace, don't you?" his mum asked, leaning towards him.

"Yea, yea, the necklace – but that was ages ago and the other stones are lost."

His stepdad looked up. "Not exactly lost – just missing," he said, "at least one of them is."

"The stone of love," said his mum. "The central stone in the necklace; that's the connection. It was once in the possession of the Rebel Prince. Maybe this new 'Prince' thinks he knows where to find it."

"So what?" Josh exclaimed. "I'm the Guardian. If the necklace is restored, it's mine. It's no use to anybody else."

"He doesn't want anyone to use it," said his mum. "He just wants to claim it for himself, like his famous ancestor. It's a very visible way of saying 'I'm in charge now!' The necklace is a promise of peace between pirates and colonists. This man doesn't want peace. So, if he gets his hands on those stones…" She looked hard at Josh and then looked away and restarted the sentence: "Let's say we must do everything to make sure that your stone is safe."

His stepdad patted him on the shoulder and stood up. "And that you're safe too, of course," he said; "especially now we know that Ronald Fleck is involved."

Josh looked up in horror. "Thanks, Dad," he said. "How much are you not telling me?"

CHAPTER THREE

J osh climbed onto the school coach; an ancient green coach, parked in the school yard, belching clouds of black smoke. He found a seat at the back next to Sandy Oldways and gazed out of the window, watching Miss Sparrow, their history teacher, flapping around in the playground, rounding up the last of her charges.

All night he'd been thinking about Megs and the Cat Lady and Fleck. That coffin thing had Fleck written all over it. Nobody knew where that little man with round spectacles had gone when he vanished after the death of Machin. Was he the 'master' the Cat Lady referred to or was that the Prince?

He stared at the seated rows of chattering heads in front of him. No one was likely to attack him on a school coach. But what about when they arrived?

"Who are we waiting for?" asked Sandy, gazing out of the window.

"No idea. I don't know half these kids. They must be from the year below us. Whew! It's stuffy in here. There's a smell of socks."

"Pirate socks," said Sandy.

"That's not very PC."

"It's a fact," Sandy whispered. His honest, freckled face turned from the window. "Haven't you noticed something?"

"What?"

"I'm the only colonist kid here."

"So? That's because a lot of your colonist friends have moved to posh schools in town."

"I preferred it when we were mixed; pirates and colonists. Now every time I walk into the classroom, someone calls out, "Kill the colonist! It never used to be like that, you know."

Josh laughed. "Why don't you thump them? You're easily the biggest kid in our class."

Sandy gazed out of the window again. "I don't fight people. I'm a vegetarian."

"Well, you don't have to eat them. Anyway, you're not a vegetarian. You're a pacifist."

"Yes, I'm probably one of those too."

Josh sighed and looked around him.

The coach was filling up. Miss Sparrow stood up front beside the driver, pursing her lips. "Jason Potts, you're late. You have kept the whole coach waiting!"

"Yes, Miss. Sorry, Miss. A bit of urgent business behind the bike sheds." He flicked back a lock of oily, black hair and winked at a few of his mates, as he edged past her towards the back of the coach.

"What about me, Miss? Have I kept the coach waiting too?"

"That's Martin Green," whispered Josh, drawing Sandy's attention to the thin, freckled boy with a pointy, insolent face who had just boarded. He was new to the school and smaller than most of his classmates, but he had a certain air of secrecy and hardness.

"Yes, you too, Martin Green."

"But you asked me to find Potts, Miss."

"So I did. Then why did you ask me? Oh, look, stop playing games with me, Green. Just find a seat. We're late enough as it is."

Green hung around up front, pretending to be looking for his friend.

"Before we start," Miss Sparrow sighed, clutching the microphone, "I am obliged to give you all a little safety demonstration. Sit down, Potts – no, not on Marianne Fairweather – there's a space at the back next to Flagsmith. What's that, Green?"

"I said 'Do you like my new sticker, Miss? Potts is wearing one too."

"Yes, very nice, Green. 'RR' But I have no idea what it means. Anyway, the bus is waiting to start."

"You don't know about RR, Miss? Everybody knows about RR!"

"Yes, yes, Green. Rupert the Rotten, of course. Now will you please sit down so that I can start my safety demonstration? You are all familiar with seatbelts, I suppose. However, I am legally obliged to show you how…"

"Not Rotten, Miss. Rupert the Rebel!" exclaimed Green, not budging. "Some people think he was the greatest pirate that ever lived. If Rupert had had his way, Miss, there wouldn't be any stinking colonists like Sandy Oldways left on this island."

A few gasps and sniggers greeted this remark. One or two boys at the back shouted out "Bring back RR!"

Miss Sparrow screwed up her face in fury. She stared at Green, who raised both hands in mock apology, and her mouth wobbled as she struggled for the appropriate punishment or put-down phrase. Several eyes glanced back at Sandy to see how he would react to the insult. Sandy stared around him in a puzzled sort of way and said nothing.

"Sit down, Green. I'll deal with you later," she snapped, stumbling backwards as the coach driver lost patience and the coach lurched into motion.

Josh looked at Sandy in disgust as Green and Potts took their places beside them in the back seat. "Nice one, Green," he muttered in the boy's ear. "I bet that's done wonders for your street cred."

"Don't tangle with him," Potts leaned over to advise his friend. "His dad's the headmaster."

"Teacher's pet, eh?" added Green.

Josh shot out an arm and Green's head sailed into the metal bar of the seat in front.

"Are they bothering you, Josh?" Miss Sparrow stood up to enquire.

"No, Miss. Green's just hit his head on the seat. He's got a nasty bump. Or perhaps that's just his nose."

There were a few laughs from Josh's friends scattered around the bus, leaving Green and Potts to vent their malice in whispers for the rest of the journey.

"What's your problem, Green?" Josh asked, when the taunting showed no signs of letting up. "What have you got against colonists? And what's all this stuff about RR?"

"Wouldn't you like to know?"

"Not really. But you seem to want to tell me, so tell me."

"You'll find out soon enough!"

The Island History Museum used to be the Chief Minister's house but, during his term of office, his stepdad had donated the building to the Ministry of Culture and moved his family to a humbler building on the opposite side of the square. The school party filed up the steps to the main entrance on the first floor where a fat, balding official in a blue uniform leaned back on his chair, using a ruler to prop his stomach against the ticket desk.

"Ah, the Sloane Academy! I was expecting you!" he said in a deep, self-satisfied voice, removing the ruler and rising wearily to his feet. "And you must be the worthy Miss Sparrow! I seem to remember you from my university days. Dear me! How times have changed! Now you are reduced to the humble task of educating the masses while I, the former minister for culture – no less – have become a mere seller of tickets."

"That's Humphrey Griffin," whispered Sandy, standing with Josh at the back of the queue. "He used to work for the Machin regime, didn't he? Before your stepdad took over?"

"He didn't have much choice," Josh whispered back. "He was minister of culture in the government before Machin. Most of his lot ended up in prison; or dead."

"Ah, Master Flagsmith," Griffin exclaimed, picking him out from the throng and provoking a few muttered remarks from Green and his pals. "The young Guardian! To what do we owe this pleasure?"

"He's with me," snapped Miss Sparrow.

"He's with you. I can see he's with you. Ah yes, indeed," said Griffin. He gave a long-suffering sigh and surveyed the crowd. "Thirty-six of you, are there?" he enquired. "All thirsty for knowledge, no doubt. You are the only visitors this morning, so take your time. The display is laid out in chronological order, ancient history in the grand hall and modern history downstairs in what used to be Reginald Machin's private apartments." He stared at the line of school pupils as if the sight of them had made him lose his appetite for life. "I suppose I'd better introduce myself," he added. "I'm Mr Humphrey Griffin, curator of this museum."

He lumbered forward and pulled open the great doors of the assembly hall. "Follow me," he said. "I'm coming with you part of the way to make sure you don't nick anything. That's what teenagers generally like to do in my experience; draw on the walls and nick things."

"I can assure you that none of my charges are like that!" exclaimed Miss Sparrow, glaring at a few teenage girls who had broken into giggles.

"Let's hang back and let this lot go ahead," whispered Josh to Sandy, pulling him back from the queue jostling to get into the hall. "They're more interested in the modern stuff downstairs. I want to find out more about the Guardian's necklace and Rupert the Rebel."

While they talked, the queue filed through into the museum. Josh noticed that the grand assembly hall upstairs with its crystal chandeliers had remained unchanged. The room had simply been partitioned by white fibre-glass screens, just above head height. One long screen ran down the centre of the room, with shorter horizontal screens attached at intervals to either side, creating square white cubicles – with the wall making up the fourth side of each cubicle. The idea was to wander through the centuries in an anti-clockwise direction, starting from the right.

"Come on, we know all this stuff," whispered Josh, entering the first cubicle containing maps and diagrams devoted to pre-history. "Are you interested in the early pirates? That's along here somewhere, I think."

"Maybe, but let's hang around for a bit. That's where the noise is coming from."

They could hear shouts and laughter echoing from halfway down the hall in front of them

"I don't think much of the partitions," murmured Sandy.

Josh grinned.

"No, but seriously. They're not sound-proofed. They are so flimsy that you could cut them with a penknife. Look!"

"No way! That's tough fibre – you'd need a sharp sword to cut through it."

"Yes. But look at the joints! I could cut through that!"

"Well, don't, anyway! Let's move on."

Halfway down the right-hand side of the hall, they reached a screened room entitled 'Pirate Voyagers of 5 BD.'

"What's BD really stand for?"

Josh stared at his friend. "Don't you know anything? BD! 'Before the disaster.' That's about four hundred years ago when the first pirate civilisation got too advanced for its own good and ended up destroying its own habitat. The great guardian, Matilda, foresaw the disaster and led a fleet of followers to settle in Amaryllis. Rupert the Rebel was one of them. In a few years they colonised every island in the western isles.

"So, the first pirates were colonists too!" crowed Sandy. "We colonists weren't the only bad guys!"

"But we got there earlier!" protested Josh. "Twenty years earlier! Come on, let's move on. It's the Rebel Prince I'm interested in."

"You mean Rupert the Rotten," said Sandy. "What's that noise?"

Josh stopped. "I didn't hear anything."

"It sounded like footsteps in the entrance lobby."

"Probably Griffin."

They skipped several more cubicles and found themselves at the end of the hall and rounding the horseshoe towards the exit. Josh could already hear his classmates leaving the assembly hall and descending in a chattering mass to the exhibition of 'Modern Times' on the floor below.

"This is more like it!" exclaimed Sandy, coming to the final exhibit entitled 'The Arrival of the Colonists'. Unlike the previous square cubicles displaying charts and photographs, this was a spacious area, full of all kinds of artefacts, including the weapons and farming tools of the early colonists as well as one complete colonist longboat mounted on the wall.

"Wow, they were a savage lot, your ancestors!" teased Josh. "Imagine them coming over in homemade boats like that, with their primitive weapons, and conquering most of the western isles, giving them stupid new colonist names like Discovery Island, Colony Island, The Last Resort. They were running out of ideas by the time they got to our island. Look at this! 'The first colonists left their lands on religious grounds. Their Flat Earth Religion was banned on the eastern continent so the believers were forced to flee from religious persecution at home and seek new lands where they could practise it on others.'

"He sounds a bit anti-colonist, the person who wrote that!"

"Well, look at them; half-naked muscle-bound thugs with huge swords, wearing metal chamber pots on their heads."

"I can't see any chamber pots!"

"I'm not joking. Look! 'Carl the Rude was famous for inventing a helmet with a brass handle, which could equally well be used for cooking and other domestic needs."

"Let's have a look at your lot, then," Sandy retorted.

"There you are! Rupert the Rotten. Well, that's what colonists call him. He's even got the letters "RR" inscribed on each sleeve."

"He looks okay, really," said Sandy. "I wonder why his head's shaven. And he's got long robes, like a monk."

"It's a painting," Josh reminded him. "Perhaps that's how he wanted to be painted."

"What about this lady by his side? She looks – well, okay. Just a painting too, I suppose."

"No, that's Matilda, the Guardian. She was gorgeous."

Josh thought of the lady he'd seen through his stone. His eyes fell on the long, golden necklace falling from her neck onto the crimson folds of her dress. "Look!"

"What am I supposed to be looking at?"

"The Guardian's necklace."

"Well, it's a necklace. More expensive than most, I suppose but–"

Josh seized his friend by the shoulder. "Take a good look at it. And then look at the cabinet display below."

"Well, there's a gold chain and – what's this? Black onyx? It looks like three, round onyx pendants; a small one on each side and a slightly larger one hanging straight down in the middle. One of them's your stone isn't it, Josh?"

"The stone of truth, yes. The one on the left, I think. But there's two other stones! The stone of love. That's the main one – and the stone of knowledge."

"What am I looking at? It's another stone. It should be here somewhere," said Sandy. "Your stepdad lent it to the museum, remember?"

"Did he? Well, it's here! Except it's a replica!" Josh looked down at a small glass-covered table close to the portrait of Matilda. "It says here," he said, reading the inscription, "'The stone of knowledge was donated to this museum by the former Chief Minister, David Flagsmith. It was recently stolen and the exhibit in this case is a replica. Signed: Humphrey Griffin, Curator.'"

"So, that's it," he thought. The stone should have been his! It belonged to the Guardian! And now his stepdad had lent it to the museum, and it was lost!

"Do you think the man calling himself the Rebel Prince was behind this?" asked Sandy.

"It has to be his work, I suppose," said Josh. He wondered if Griffin kept a record of visitors. That would be one way to trace the thief.

They had almost reached the exit now and heard the click of a key turning in the lock.

"That's our exit," whispered Josh.

"How do you know it's not the way we came in?"

"The sound came from our right. Didn't you hear it?" Josh shrugged. It didn't make sense. If Griffin wanted them to go, surely, he wouldn't block their exit?

Seconds later they both heard the creak of the entrance door opening and the sound of footsteps entering the hall. They heard a whispered conversation between two visitors, followed by the sound of a second key turning in a second lock.

"If one of them's Griffin," whispered Sandy, "why has he locked both doors?"

"No idea!"

Josh looked at Sandy. He did have an idea after all, and his legs started to shake. He felt another fit coming on and felt in his pocket to grip his stone. The huge hall had become a locked room. Neither of the two visitors sounded like Griffin.

"Who else would have the keys?" asked Sandy.

"Sh! Listen!" Josh's heart beat faster as he listened to the footsteps on the other side of the partition. The visitors hadn't left the first cubicle yet. They seemed to be taking their time.

"He's in here somewhere," said a cold voice. "He's got a friend with him. They're probably bricking it. Isn't that the phrase they use nowadays, these young people?"

Josh knew that voice. He looked around him at the bare walls with windows set well above head height. There was nowhere to hide, no means of escape. He felt like a trapped mouse awaiting the slow, sinuous approach of a boa constrictor.

"They can hear you," growled the other voice coming from a great height.

Josh looked at Sandy who leant against the wall as if only the solid stone could save him.

"I want them to hear me," Fleck was saying. "They'll find the exit door is locked so there's nothing they can do about it. I think it's time to get that stone. He'll give it to you, Osborne. All it needs is a bit of mindless violence; you owe me, remember for getting you out of that nice prison."

Osborne! Josh knew Osborne. He used to work for Machin. He shivered at the memory.

"It's my job, innit?" said the rough voice, "Let's go after them."

"No hurry," said the first voice. "They'll wait for us."

The footsteps reached the second cubicle. Josh put a hand on Sandy's shoulder and they both froze. Soon only a thin partition would divide them.

Josh could picture them; a giant twice his size accompanied by a small man in round spectacles. The small man frightened him the most. Ancient weapons hung on the wall if they had the guts to use them. He shuddered. With Osborne around, it would be like firing darts at a tank.

"Can't you do something with your stone?" whispered Sandy. "Like mess with his mind? That's what you did with Machin."

"Forget it!" whispered Josh. "Fleck doesn't have the kind of mind you can mess with."

The footsteps were moving on now. Josh put his finger to his lips and gestured to Sandy to move towards the locked exit; for a second, as their paths crossed, the shadows of their pursuers showed up on the partition wall.

Where now? They had come to the last partition and had nowhere left to hide.

"Quick, Sandy!" Josh whispered. "Pass me your penknife!"

"What for?"

Josh grabbed it and ran a hand along the partition, feeling for the weak point at the seam.

The voices sounded further away now. That meant they'd reached the end of the hall and would soon be heading round in their direction.

"What are you trying to do?"

"Cut through the seam. You said it was easy."

"But why?"

Josh shrugged. "Buy us a bit of time."

The voices got closer.

The knife slid through the join in the partition, enabling them to pull back one side and slip through. Now the two boys stood at the point where they'd come in, hearing footsteps halfway down the other side of the hall.

They stared at each other. Whichever way you looked, the bare walls offered nowhere to hide. Josh had a sudden thought and patted his pockets. He pulled out his phone.

Sandy shook his head vigorously. "Don't do it, Josh. It'll bring them here in seconds."

The footsteps had reached the cubicle they'd just left.

Josh tapped Sandy on the shoulder and pointed to the wall beside the entrance where a narrow archway led down to the toilets.

Sandy hesitated, "They'll find us."

"Better than nothing. Quick. You go first."

He followed Sandy through the archway and closed the door behind him. There was no lock but he still felt a degree safer than upstairs in that echoing hall.

Just then he heard a roar from the far side of the partition. "Blast them! They've slipped through!"

Josh gave Sandy a shove. "Quick! Downstairs! Let's check the toilets." He heard the crashing sound of a heavy body breaking through the partition. Osborne didn't bother with penknives.

Sandy stood at the bottom of the steps, in the narrow hallway outside the toilets.

"What are you doing?" asked Josh.

"This door leads to the floor below. It's only thin. I thought maybe we could break it down."

Josh held up a restraining hand. He thought he heard footsteps approaching from the other side. He listened. The footsteps had reached the door. He heard the click of a key. He relaxed and gave Sandy a quick thumbs up.

"I don't know where I put those wretched keys," grumbled a familiar voice. Humphrey Griffin stood framed in the doorway. "The main door is never supposed to be locked," he muttered to himself. He looked up and noticed the two boys for the first time. "You'll have to follow me through the side exit on the ground floor."

The voice of Fleck rang out from the floor above. "Never mind, Osborne, we can pick them off any time we want. The boy's going on a voyage soon. That should be interesting, eh?"

"That was Fleck," panted Josh, barging past Griffin with Sandy close behind. "He's up there with a thug called Osborne! Call the police!"

"Fleck indeed! I'm beginning to see what you mean." Griffin's eyes widened as he struggled to lock the door behind him. Josh could tell from the way he rolled his eyes that he knew all about Fleck. Anyone who had worked for Reginald Machin knew about Fleck.

"And let's get well clear of this museum!" Josh advised. "Osborne could break down this door in seconds. Where's the ground floor exit?"

Humphrey Griffin soon stood beside them outside his museum, staring up at the steps leading to the main entrance where he expected the dreaded Fleck to emerge. He wrung his hands in a froth of indecision. "Yes, yes. Go back in there and ring the police. And then get out of here quick! Or get away first and then ring the police. Oh dear, Oh dear! Ronald Fleck! I thought we had seen the last of him."

Globules of sweat glistened on his brow as his eyes darted from left to right, wondering where best to hide his ample frame. At that moment an exasperated Miss Sparrow raced towards the steps, darting furious looks in all directions. "Where are those boys?" she screeched. "We're late enough as it is."

Humphrey Griffin came to a decision. "Well, I will do as you wisely suggested, my boys, and make myself scarce. I see no pressing need to detain you any further. Your charioteer seems to be in somewhat of a hurry."

Josh and Sandy ran towards the coach. Miss Sparrow caught them climbing on board and pressed two library tickets into Josh's hand. "Your stepdad's just phoned," she snapped. "He says he'll meet you in one hour on the steps of the library."

"The library?" said Josh, accepting the tickets with a grin. "That's cool!"

"The library? That's cool!" mimicked a mocking voice from the coach.

"That's Green," Sandy shouted after him as they raced across the darkening square.

"Who cares? He's not Fleck. Follow me!"

A continuous sound of police sirens echoed in their wake.

CHAPTER FOUR

They rushed to the central library, a narrow timber-framed town house stooped and bent with age, on the opposite side of the square. The door sprang open the moment they pressed the bell and a small man in a green velvet jacket and bow tie welcomed them inside. His head was bald, apart from a few white wisps of hair on either side, and he greeted them with a teasing smile.

"You're Josh Flagsmith, and you, I presume, must be Sandy." As he said this, his smile etched creases at the corners of his mouth. "Please follow me into my office."

They stepped into a musty smell of dust and floor polish and fried food.

"It used to be a guesthouse, Mr Flagsmith," explained the librarian. Not all the stock has been catalogued as yet," he added with a sigh. "Anyway, you'd better come through."

"How did you know my name?" asked Josh

"Everyone knows the boy with the stone. May I see it?"

Josh shrugged at Sandy and fished an onyx stone from his pocket.

"I see. A pretty object but not for me, I'm afraid. Stones like that can only get you into trouble. There's enough trouble around this part of town already."

"What do you mean?"

"Your dad ran this island for a year, I believe?"

"My stepdad."

"Stepdad, is he? Of course. It's all right for some."

They followed him down a narrow, carpeted corridor lined with books from floor to ceiling into a large room, dimly lit by a single chandelier, where books lined the walls and lay in piles on the floor. A huge desk strewn with papers and periodicals occupied the remaining space. The librarian picked his way with care to his seat on the other side of his desk and smiled at them like a well-fed tabby cat.

"The books which I've had time to catalogue up to now all have titles beginning with A," he explained, with half an eye on the uncompleted crossword lying on his desk. "I don't suppose I can interest you in armadillos or aardvarks? No? Then I think you'll find what you're after on the fourth floor which starts with the letter R; R for Rupert. Did I say 'starts'? I mean you'll find anything at that end of the alphabet, but in no particular order. I am sorry I can't direct you to a lift because there isn't one. You'll find the stairs on your left. I wouldn't advise you to place too much weight on the banisters. Nasty accidents have been known to happen."

"Thanks." The boys jostled to get out of the room and up the stairs, casting a backward glance at the librarian who'd returned to his crossword.

"Do you think he's one of them?" whispered Josh, turning back to Sandy as he reached the landing on the second floor. "I think we'd better watch our backs just in case."

"He was a bit strange," Sandy agreed. "How did he know our names?"

"I don't know. I suppose he knows my stepdad. He seemed bitter about something."

They climbed two more narrow staircases to the fourth floor, a low-ceilinged attic room with gabled windows overlooking the street.

Sandy settled into a large glossy book with romantic illustrations entitled "The Life and Times of a Rotter," and made himself comfortable in an antique armchair in a corner next to one of the windows. He showed Josh the picture of a banquet. Rupert, an oily rascal with curling, black hair, was presenting a steaming dish to his parents, King Cuthbert the Clueless and Queen Agnes the Appalling.

"Look. He was more rotten than I thought. They're all sitting round this huge casserole, right? And Queen Agnes is saying, 'Rupert, I'm glad you've agreed to be reconciled with your older brother, "and Rupert's saying, 'Oh yes, Mama. I thought he tasted delicious.'"

Josh pushed the book away. He lay sprawled on the floor leafing through a leather-bound volume called *The Official History of Colony Island, Book 3 - The Arrival of the Colonists.* "Your book's obviously written by a colonist," he said over his shoulder. "I wouldn't believe half of it. It says here, 'According to the *Piratica*, Rupert was provoked into action when the colonists attempted to take over the island.' Listen to this: 'By his own followers, Rupert was known as Rupert the Rebel.'"

"RR, Rupert the Rebel!"

"Yes, he had a point, when you think about it. It was his island and your lot invaded it."

"Don't blame me. I wasn't born then. What have you found about Matilda?"

"I haven't got to that bit yet. There are pages and pages of this stuff. Here it is: 'Matilda proposed to share power with the colonists. Not many pirates supported her at first. Rupert wanted to drive the colonists out. Since the pirates were outnumbered and had an inferior army, he hatched up a scheme to poison all the wells in The Last Resort where the colonist army had their base.'"

"With what?"

"*Oblivia preciosa*, of course; don't say you've forgotten the oblivion flower! That's when Matilda and Rupert came to blows."

"Any mention of the stones?"

"Yes, Rupert tried to grab the Guardian's necklace from Matilda at the Treaty of the River Snake, but he came away with just one pendant – the stone of love. Matilda had poured all her remaining power into that necklace and when it was broken, she died soon after; some say from an epileptic fit…"

"Josh?"

"Yes?"

"Nothing. It's not important."

"Go on. Say it."

"You have epilepsy, don't you? I mean, you did have?"

"I still do. But my stone helps me control it."

"Is that what your stone's for? I thought it was for visions and stuff."

"The stone's like a computer; it works like 'ask Agnes'; except the advice it gives comes from BD – the age before the disaster – when they were much more advanced than we are now."

Josh wriggled into a more comfortable position on the floor and went on reading. "Hang on!" he exclaimed. "A lot of this paragraph has been underlined. I wonder who else has been reading this book."

"Don't they list the names of borrowers on the inside cover?"

"Of course. There's a whole list of names here but the last one – you guessed it! It's Catharine Cattermole."

"She must be interested in that stone, I suppose."

"Wake up, Sandy! We knew that!"

"Oh yes, of course."

"But she signed this last week. Good news. It means that the Prince hasn't found it."

"Does it say what happened to the stone?"

"Wait! Here it is! 'The Treaty of the River Snake. Nobody knows what happened to the stone of love which Rupert seized from Matilda. After the Treaty, Rupert ordered his army to attack Matilda's forces. The colonists went to Matilda's aid and his own army was forced to retreat to his castle, north of the River Snake, where he died a horrible death, poisoned by one of his servants. Much of his baggage was lost in the retreat, including the stone of love. Some of his treasures have been recovered by Professor Sedgeworth in his excavations around the Castle Rock area, which is all that remains of Rupert's castle, but the stone was not among them."

"I know Professor Sedgeworth!" said Sandy suddenly. "He's a neighbour. He's an old bloke. Well, I don't really know him. I just see him pottering in his garden sometimes. I didn't know he was an archae…archae…well, someone who digs things up and stuff."

They heard the sound of a ringing doorbell four floors below. "That's got to be my dad!" said Josh. He led the way, racing down two steps at a time.

"Have a safe journey!" said the librarian, following them to the door. Josh didn't think he sounded very convincing.

CHAPTER FIVE

J osh's stepdad sat in his hatchback outside the library. He started up the engine the moment he saw them. "A bit of a rumpus going on at home at the moment," he shouted out of the window. "Miss Cattermole's vanished."

Josh exchanged glances with Sandy. "From where, Dad?" he asked.

"The local prison. A van drove up and two men dressed as warders fixed a charge to the cell wall. Half the prison's in ruins. Most of the prisoners just hung around, waiting to be put back in their cells. A few brave souls escaped but got picked up straightaway. Not the Cat Lady. Anyway, get in the van. Sandy in the front. He's got longer legs. It's going to be a long journey, I'm afraid. Police checks everywhere. Not that they will do any good. A lot of these people hate the police more than they hate the Cat Lady and her gang."

"You heard about Fleck?" asked Josh.

"Heard it on the radio. That's why I came to collect you. We've got to get you out of here."

A large crowd in the central square blocked their progress, carrying banners and chanting "Power to the Pirates! RR, Rupert the Rebel!" and "Give us our homes back!" Angry faces loomed close to the windscreen, backing off as the car nosed its way ahead.

"I'm afraid I'm responsible for that slogan," said David Flagsmith. "A lot of pirates who lost their homes under Machin never got them back again or received proper compensation."

"But that's unfair!" exclaimed Josh.

"So was the alternative. Anyway, Machin left us bankrupt. Let's move on before they recognise me."

Josh thought about the Cat Lady. "How's Megs taking it, Dad?"

"She doesn't know yet. Best not to tell her for the moment, don't you think?"

"What do we do when she finds out?"

"That's the point, Josh. We've got to get you and Megs off this island. You too, Sandy. They may use you to get to Josh. I've explained all this to your parents. It's all to do with this damned necklace. I'm not a pirate, as you know, but I guess this man needs it to prove he's the Rebel Prince – finishing the job his ancestor left undone."

Josh thought of Fleck's last words. How had he known Josh would be going on a voyage? Anyway, he wasn't leaving the island yet. No way! He had to find those stones first!

"You've gone very quiet, Josh; is something bothering you?"

"No, Dad," he said. "By the way, we found out about the stone of knowledge. You lent it to the museum."

"Yes. I thought it would be safe there for the time being."

"We saw it."

"Good."

"Except it was a replica."

His stepdad shot forward in his seat. "Oh."

"The original stone has been stolen."

"Damn!"

Seeing the lines of worry on his stepdad's face, Josh couldn't get angry with him. But he'd really messed up. "What if the

Prince has got it?" he asked.

His stepdad swivelled round in his seat to speak to him. "It's not the Prince," he said. "I'm sure about that. I spoke to the Cat Lady this morning before she escaped. It's pretty clear from what she said that they haven't got any of those stones yet."

"Don't you have to sign in when you visit the museum?" asked Josh.

"I suppose so. I certainly had to. Why?"

"We could ask for the visitor list on the day it was stolen."

"Good idea. I'll look into it."

"Good."

"I'm sure we'll recover it."

"Good."

"Your safety's the important thing, of course."

"Thanks, Dad. You're on the wrong side of the road."

"Oh yes."

On the outskirts of town, they encountered their first police check. Men in uniforms strode up and down and looked busy. One or two white vans were stationed at the side of the road, their owners muttering among themselves on the grass verge while their belongings were sniffed by tracker dogs. The police recognised Josh's stepdad and waved him on his way.

As they travelled in silence along an empty stretch of road, Josh thought about that stone of love. "I'm not ready to leave the island yet," he told his stepdad. "I've got to speak to Professor Sedgeworth."

"Sedgeworth? The name seems familiar. What's he got to do with anything? Look, Josh, it's not safe for you to go anywhere on this island at the moment."

"He's an archaeologist," explained Josh. "He's been looking for Rupert's stone. I need to know…I mean, we all need to know if he's found it."

"It's not a good idea, Josh. I can't risk it."

"I could phone him," suggested Sandy.

"I suppose that's possible. Do you have his number?"

"I can phone my parents. He's a neighbour."

The phone call lasted a long time. After the initial query, it mainly consisted of Sandy saying "Yes, Mum…all right, Mum," and "I see." He put the phone down and said nothing.

"Well?" asked Josh, half guessing the answer.

"My mum says there's been an accident. His house is surrounded by police."

"We'd better go there," said Josh's stepdad. "It's not far out of our way and maybe you can drop in on your parents and say your goodbyes while you're at it."

After a short drive, they pulled into a leafy avenue of large, square colonist houses, three on either side of the road. The police had cordoned off the middle house on the left. Sandy hurried into his parents' house, next door. Josh followed, leaving his stepdad to talk with two police officers bending over the lawn, picking up and bagging stray objects hidden in the grass.

They soon piled back into the hatchback while Sandy's parents stood outside their front door, waving goodbye. Josh saw the concern on his stepdad's face. He held up a charred brass circlet which he tossed on the back seat of the car. "Let's get out of here," he muttered, revving up the engine.

"What did you find, Dad?" asked Josh.

"A bomb. Poor Mr Sedgeworth. There can't be anything much worse than being attacked for information you haven't got. They made a complete mess of…well, his cellar among other things. They must have led him down there because they knew the thick walls would muffle the sound. Your mother was the only one to hear it, apparently," he said to Sandy. "Fortunately, we have no way of knowing what they did to Mr Sedgeworth. The bomb didn't leave much in the way of evidence."

"Poor old Sedgeworth!" murmured Sandy.

"Why did they kill him?" asked Josh.

"Probably because he couldn't tell them anything. I don't know. And to make sure he couldn't give them away."

"So they haven't got the stone of love but they are willing to kill for it."

"That about sums it up."

Josh picked up the brass circlet and held it up for Sandy to see.

"It's open at the moment," his stepdad warned. "Don't close it or you will never get it apart again. Whoever made this won't be too happy to know it's fallen into enemy hands."

"How does it open, Dad?"

"It doesn't, unless the owner is forced to commit suicide by blowing himself up. Take a closer look. The instructions are quite clear."

Josh examined the circlet with its four variously coloured steel balls evenly spaced around the rim. On each ball he saw an etched inscription; "Obedience brings pleasure...disobedience brings pain...the ultimate sacrifice brings relief..." The last inscription told its own tale. The ball containing the explosive device was a blackened lump of jagged steel. Finally, a yellow ball contained the maker's logo – a smiley face with a twisted smile.

"How does this thing work, Dad?"

"You see the little steel loops running round the top edge of the circlet? That's for attaching a chain-mail helmet. The helmet contains ear-pieces through which the commands are transmitted and a mouth-piece for responding to the commands. Waves of pleasure or pain are then sent like shock waves through the body by the person sitting at the controls, probably in a comfortable room on the island of Windfree."

"The smile's a bit lopsided. It reminds me of Fleck," said Sandy.

"Ronald Fleck!" muttered Josh. "Who else would dream up such a nasty device?"

They were still ten miles from home and it was beginning to grow dark. Josh thought about poor Mr Sedgeworth and the cruel power of the brass circlet. He had guessed that Fleck was behind it. Could you free yourself from the circlet without blowing yourself up? His stepdad would be able to check that in his laboratory. Meanwhile, Rupert's stone probably still lay in the place where Rupert lost it 400 years ago. But maybe combing the site for a small onyx stone was not the answer. Could they find out how Rupert spent his last days? When exactly did he lose the stone and where was he when he lost it? Those were the questions people asked him every time he lost something. Not that it helped much. His mum usually said 'Keep looking, because it must be somewhere,' but that didn't help much either.

Josh's mind returned to the present; sitting in the car, rolling through the countryside in silence on the last leg of their journey. But it was not completely silent, any more than a kitchen is silent when the dishwasher and washing machine are whirring in the background. So it was with the hum of the car engine and a monotonous, stifled snoring that came from the pile of rugs in the luggage space behind him. It dawned on him that this sound warranted an explanation. It wasn't just the normal mechanical sound you would expect from an old car. It was an altogether more human sound, like an old man with a very bad cold. "What's that noise, Dad?" he asked.

"Oh, that's Gregory."

"What's he doing in our car, Dad?"

"Before coming to meet you, I received a call to pick him up from his quarters - you know, the park beyond our house that used to be called 'the other side of the world.' He's in a bit of a bad way. He can't hear us, can he?"

"I think he's sound asleep, Dad."

"Good, then I can tell you he's not as young as he used to be, and the climate here doesn't suit him as well as Amaryllis. I think he's caught a bit of a cold. Let's hope it's nothing worse. I thought I'd bring him home and settle him down beside a nice fire. Megs can nurse him back to health. She'd like that. Take her mind off other things."

"Who's Gregory?" asked Sandy, turning round in the front seat.

"He's an extremely large and totally harmless tiger," explained Josh. "A talking tiger. He's one of the very few talking animals that still exist in the world. He's from Amaryllis. That's where Megs and I first met him."

"I've heard about talking animals, but I've never met one," said Sandy. "Pirates are supposed to be able to understand what they say, but I'm not a pirate." After a long pause, he added, "I'm glad about the harmless bit," and sat up very straight and still, as if trying to airbrush the tiger's existence out of his mind.

When they reached the house, they left Gregory sleeping at the back of the station wagon while Josh broke the news to a delighted Megs. Everyone got involved, stoking a fire in the kitchen, throwing down blankets for a makeshift bed and preparing him a meaty broth. Getting him out of the car was another matter. Since he was too heavy to lift, it was left to Megs to sit beside him in the back of the car and stroke his head and coax him into wakefulness until he found the energy to rise onto his forelegs and heave his body out onto the ground.

CHAPTER SIX

Josh winked at Sandy and hung back in the hallway, letting his stepdad go first. His mum looked dangerously animated. She dashed everywhere, running upstairs to sort out a bed for Sandy, then down again to see to a casserole steaming in the oven, then back to the dining room on the floor above, carrying a tray of plates and cutlery. She kept pushing black strands of hair from her flushed face. He couldn't tell if she was pleased or annoyed at all this multi-tasking. He thought it could go either way.

"This couldn't have come at a worse time," she confided to Josh, throwing an arm over his shoulder. "I've been on duty at the hospital all day. They're terribly busy – well, they always are – and they may need me again tonight. So, if I have to leave the table at any point, I hope you'll vouch for my absence?" She tweaked his ear and he nodded.

"I'll help you with that!" called Josh's stepdad, waving a hand at the tray she was carrying towards the stairs.

"Yes, dear. I don't know if you remember that you invited the captain and his mate to dinner."

Tonight?"

"Yes, tonight. And that nice young research assistant."

"John Bosworthy?"

"You invited him too, apparently."

"Right," he said, relieving her of the tray. "Here, Josh, help your mum with the knives and forks. Sandy! Plates. You know where to find them. I won't be a moment."

"Unless your dad has invited any more people that I don't know about," she said, "I make it eight of us plus a tiger. I'm going to leave you and Sandy to sort out the dining room. You'll need to find an extra table from somewhere. The small table from our bedroom will do. And chairs, glasses, what else?"

"Don't worry, we'll sort it out, Mrs Flagsmith."

"I'm sure you will, Sandy," said Josh's mum with a sudden smile, running a hand through his thatch of fair hair. Thank goodness we have one practical person around!"

"What about me, Mum?" asked Josh.

"Well, practical isn't the word that springs to mind but you're not so bad either, Josh."

"How's Megs?" he asked.

"She'll be a lot better now that she's got Gregory to look after. See for yourself. You too, Sandy."

Sandy hung his head. "If you don't mind, Mrs Flagsmith, I'm not really into tigers."

Josh hid a smile.

"Don't mind Gregory," said his mum. "I promise you, Sandy, talking tigers are not the same thing as normal tigers. Not the same thing at all."

Sandy looked unconvinced. "The problem is, Mrs Flagsmith, that I'm not a pirate so I don't understand that sort of animal. If he talks and I don't know what he's saying, that might make him angry."

Josh's mum came closer and put her arms round him. "Don't be silly! Gregory has lived around people all his life. Just stroke his fur. He'll like that. What's the matter? Poor boy! You've gone white. Well, I really don't blame you. But he's a very old tiger and there's not much more he can do at the moment than lie by the fire and sleep. Josh, take Sandy into the kitchen with you and introduce him to Gregory."

Josh had had enough. He pulled Sandy into the kitchen before he had time to resist.

Megs sat on the floor, absorbed and contented, stroking the tiger's ears.

"Hi, Megs. I've brought Sandy to see Gregory. He's a bit nervous of tigers."

Megs' eyes sparkled. "Hi, Sandy," she said. "It must be frightening if you're not a pirate and can't tell the difference between Gregory and a normal tiger. Don't make fun of him, Josh! I'd be scared out of my mind. Come and sit beside me, Sandy. That's right. Don't be afraid. He may snuffle and roar a bit but that just means he is trying to tell you something. Now, I'm going to put your hand on his fur. That's right...and there you are! You're stroking him!"

Gregory opened one sleepy eye and stirred feebly into life. Josh noticed how much older and thinner he looked than when they first met on the isle of Amaryllis. "How are you feeling, Gregory?"

"Much better, thank-you. Who's this charming young man who's stroking me? I must say he's very good at it."

Sandy stumbled backwards in shock.

"Don't laugh, Josh." Megs protested. She grabbed Sandy's arm. "He says you're very charming and he likes the way you stroke him." Sandy began to smile. He replaced his hand on the tiger's back and stroked the thick fur with increasing confidence, even feeling bold enough to change position so that he could stroke the tiger's neck and legs.

"Now give him a bit of this. Turn over, Gregory. It's time for your ointment."

Sandy poured some foul-smelling liquid from Megs' bottle into the palm of his hand and rubbed it gently and methodically into the tiger's upturned chest.

"I do like this young man," said Gregory. "I could almost eat him. Can you tell him that?"

"Which bit?" asked Megs.

"Oh, all of him."

Megs thumped him on the shoulder. "You know that's not what I meant!"

Sandy went very still as the tiger hung out his tongue and started licking his face. "What's he saying?" he asked.

Josh laughed. "He says he can't get enough of you."

Sandy put a hand to his cheek where the tiger had licked him. "Why does he take so long to say it? Is that normal with talking animals?"

"That's Gregory!" said Megs.

The tiger stirred again. "Is this young man coming with us?" he purred

"Coming where?" asked Josh.

"Why, to Amaryllis!"

Josh threw a questioning glance at Megs. Who said anything about Amaryllis? That was miles away! He wouldn't find those stones in Amaryllis! Suddenly, the conversation in the room seemed far away and irrelevant, like words coming to him from beyond a glass wall.

He heard Megs saying, "Your mum says Gregory can come if he's well enough."

He vaguely nodded.

"The air on this island is too cold for me," Gregory was complaining. "It's given me a spot of bronchitis. Once I get back to the warmth of Amaryllis, I'll soon be running around and roaring like a true tiger. I'm feeling better already. Look, I'll show you!"

Josh sat up. "No, Gregory! Please don't!" He and Megs cried with a single breath, casting an anxious glance at Sandy.

"Don't what?" asked Sandy, looking around him with wide eyes. He got up with an exaggerated air of confidence and walked off to help Josh's mother with the dinner preparations while Josh and Megs sprawled around the fire at Gregory's side.

Josh seized his moment to ask what was on his mind. "Tell me, Gregory, do you remember anything about Rupert the Rotten? I mean was he as rotten as some people say?"

The tiger said nothing at first. He lifted his great head in the air and stared into space in an effort to remember things that happened a very long time ago. His answer came in a slow stream of snuffles, whines and muffled roars:

"I was a very young tiger at that time. All I remember is a nice young man, with dark, silky hair. That was before he had it all cut off. He was wearing some kind of cloak and flashing a sword. Yes, I remember him as handsome and smiling, with gentle eyes. Magnetic they were, those eyes. Many people used to say that. The one thing I remember is that he patted me on the head and told me I was the most beautiful tiger he had ever seen. I remember my mother was enormously pleased. That little incident, trifling though it may seem, was almost enough to persuade her to take Rupert's side in the war with Matilda. Then again, that was probably what he was after." He let out a mournful, sighing yawn and relapsed into his memories.

"Gregory?" asked Megs.

"Yes, young lady?"

"What do think really happened to the stone Rupert stole from Matilda?"

"People always say that it got lost with the rest of his baggage after that famous battle."

"But why didn't he wear it round his neck, like any normal person? After all it was very important for him."

"Maybe he did. Who knows?"

"In that case," suggested Josh, "it would still have been round his neck when he died. So the couple that poisoned him would have been the most likely people to steal it."

"You'd think so, wouldn't you? They are rumoured to have fled to Discovery Island. They'd have died a long time ago, being humans. Where their descendants are today, who knows?"

Discovery Island! Just across the water. That's where he had to go – not Amaryllis! "Do you remember their names?" he asked.

"Yes, Grimshaw. The couple were called Grimshaw. You might try asking the raven, Crackjaw. He's not a very amiable fellow but he lives on Discovery Island and he's the oldest of the lot of us. If anyone can tell you, it's Crackjaw. If he's in the mood, that is."

"Where will we find him?" asked Megs.

"Oh, flying around. He still flies around a bit, I'm told. Now if you don't mind, I usually like to take a walk around at this time of night. There are certain things that a tiger needs to do that can't be done in a house, if you know what I mean. Perhaps that nice young man could open the door for me and ensure that it stays open on my return."

Josh found Sandy alone, tidying up the mess his mum had left in the kitchen, He blushed with pride at being asked to act as Gregory's helper. Josh went upstairs to tackle his mum about Amaryllis. He found her laying the two tables in the sitting room.

"I didn't know we were going to Amaryllis, mum!" Josh protested.

His mum abandoned her work and came over and put her arm over his shoulder. "I know, Josh," she said. "I was going to tell you, but things are happening so quickly. I'm just scared at the thought of losing you again. It seems so soon after the last time."

"Do you know when we're leaving, Mum?"

"I think that's what this meeting is all about. It's not going to be like the last time, I can tell you. A pirate ship is coming to collect you. How about that? And we're assembling a team to go with you. That captain you met at Northwoods. Remember him?

He's here with his sergeant. The captain will be running the team. And Sandy and Megs are going with you, and Gregory. You'll hear all about it tonight."

"Great!"

Josh forced a smile. He needed to be free. He liked the idea of the captain joining them but he wouldn't find those stones in Amaryllis. "I need to go to Discovery Island," he said.

"You'll be stopping there. You'll be stopping at all the islands on route. It will be the experience of a lifetime!"

Great! he thought. Well, Fleck said it would be interesting.

His mum looked at her watch as the doorbell sounded. "Exactly eight o'clock," she whispered. "That's the military for you! Look Josh, would you be an angel and…?"

Punctuality was not a piratical virtue. Josh rushed downstairs to find the Captain standing bright-eyed and smiling, with a rucksack dangling from one hand and a gift of tall peonies in the other. Jenkins stood behind him, with a broad grin and a much larger rucksack at his feet.

After a noisy round of greetings, and a gasp of thanks for the flowers from his mum, and the arrival of an apologetic John Bosworthy, and a scraping of chairs as they all found their places at the table, the atmosphere quietened down as they all got stuck into their food. Josh's mum sat at the head of the rickety table by the door, tossing back her silky black hair as she laughed at the antics of Sergeant Jenkins, who sat on her right, next to Megs, pulling faces and cracking jokes throughout the meal. Josh felt his mother's hand resting on his shoulder from time to time as if to remind him that he was going away. He kept an eye on his stepdad, at the far end of the two tables, talking to the captain about the arrangements for the voyage. It felt different from his last journey. He didn't have to fear for his life, with the captain in charge, but he knew he'd never be safe unless he could find those stones. He needed a bit of freedom to do that!

At a wink from the captain, Jenkins sat bolt upright, put on his serious face and began the meeting. "Right, let's get started, then. I've only got one question. Why a pirate ship? Them boats aren't the quickest way to travel."

"I do like the idea of a pirate ship," put in John Bosworthy. You could tell from his eager smile that he was up for this adventure. "But it does seem a strangely conspicuous way of travelling."

"I must say that I wondered about that," said the captain, setting down his knife and fork and looking at each of Josh's parents in turn, "but then again, I'm not clear about our mission, so let's start with that."

"The mission," said David Flagsmith, "is to get these kids safely to Amaryllis."

"Right. That's clear enough. So why not tonight? Boat to Crown Colony. Helicopter to Amaryllis. Or do I detect mission creep?"

"It's all to do with this wretched stone," David Flagsmith explained. "The enemy will go to any lengths to obtain it. But in a pirate ship? A ceremonial ship that carries the pirate Guardian to his old home in Amaryllis. That's different. The man who calls himself the Rebel Prince would lose all credibility if he attacked that ship."

The captain took a piece of paper from his pocket and unfolded it on the table. "But we're not just going to Amaryllis, are we? Discovery Island, Crown Colony, Humphrey's Island, Windfree…It's quite an itinerary."

Josh leaned forward, absorbing every word.

"The ceremonial journey," his stepdad explained, "takes place every five years and includes stops at all the islands that lie on our route."

"But what's so special about Amaryllis?" asked Josh. "I mean, when I find those stones…" He blushed and started again. "I mean if I find the other stones, what happens then?"

The captain tapped the table. "I'd like to follow that question with another of my own," he said. "What is this journey really about? Are we trying to get this lad to a place of safety or are we looking for a few ancient stones?"

In the silence that followed, Josh felt the atmosphere in the room weighing him down.

Clutching the stone in his pocket, he had a sudden vision of the Prince holding out the necklace in front of a cheering army and vowing to fulfil Rupert's promise, destroying the fragile peace that existed between pirates and colonists. "We have to do both!" he burst out. "We have to go on that journey and we have to find those stones! If the Prince gets them, he'll win over half the pirate world and start another war!"

The captain held his gaze for a long time and then slowly nodded. "I saw what happened at Northwoods," he said, "so I see where you're coming from. We have to do both, then," he said, "so, what's the answer to that other question? Why Amaryllis? Is that where you expect to find these other stones?"

His dad opened his mouth to reply but his mum held up a hand to stop him. "I'm from Amaryllis myself," she said – looking hard at her husband – " and some of you may find our ways a bit strange. But the Temple of Harmony is the most sacred place in the pirate world. And if we can restore the Guardian's necklace and place it there, where Matilda always intended it to be placed, the battle with Rupert the Rebel is finally over."

"You mean that the man calling himself Rupert's heir will give up the fight?" asked the captain.

"That, or more likely, lose a large part of his support," suggested David Flagsmith. "Orthodox pirates will cease to believe in him."

"Does that mean I have to give up my stone?" asked Josh.

His mum smiled. "You won't need it anymore," she said. Your epilepsy will be cured. Is that such a bad thing?"

Josh smiled. He felt he ought to be pleased. But he'd learned how to handle his epilepsy and he didn't feel so sure about parting with his stone.

The captain looked across at his mum and nodded. "Now that I understand that there's a man calling himself 'the Rebel prince' who is after these stones," he said "and – if he gets them – plans to call his followers to arms, well…what can I say? We must find them! And for the sake of this young man here, I'd say we should find them fast!"

Josh looked up. "Grimshaw!" he exclaimed. "Grimshaw is the name of the couple who last saw Rupert alive. And we know he always wore the stone of love around his neck. So, they're the ones who must have stolen it."

"How do we know that?"

"Because they were the couple that poisoned him."

"That does make a lot of sense, Josh," his mother commented. "And once you've got the stone of love, it will lead you to that other stone. Do we know anything about this couple?"

"According to Gregory, they fled to Discovery Island."

"That's the first island on your route! Well, I think it would be safe for you to stop off at Discovery Island," his mum suggested, raising a questioning eyebrow at his dad. "I mean, providing the captain's with you."

"And we need to speak to Crackjaw," Josh said, turning to his mum. "He's a raven who still lives on the island and he's the oldest living creature."

"I don't know about hunting for tame ravens," said the captain, "but we'll follow every lead these young tearaways suggest – under strict supervision, mind. What other plans do you have in mind for tracing the descendants of these Grimshaws?"

"We could try the library," suggested Josh, "or the public record office, the telephone book…I don't know…"

"Not with me you couldn't!" said the captain firmly. "As soon as we get off that boat, there will be spies out looking for you. You don't go anywhere in public, my lad. Not while I'm in command. And that goes for Megs and Sandy too."

"The captain's right, Josh," said his stepdad. "You can't go anywhere unguarded. And, by the way, if the Grimshaws are still on the island, their ancestors probably changed their name to escape the purges. I've got a contact for you that might help; Frederic Forbes. He used to be a history teacher on the island. I'll give his contact details to the captain so that he can set up the meeting, preferably on the boat."

The captain smiled. He turned to Josh's stepdad. "Is it true that Magnus Maxtrader is coming on this trip too?" he asked.

"Not Magnus himself. His marketing executive, Tufton Pims," explained David Flagsmith. I couldn't turn him down because Magnus himself is sponsoring the voyage. But I wouldn't trust him. Rumour has it he's got business dealings with the man calling himself the Rebel Prince."

"Does Magnus have dealing with the Prince too?" asked Josh's mum.

"Who knows? His business empire has grown so big nowadays that he probably doesn't know himself. But Tufton is up to his eyes in it, I'd say. I suggest…What's that noise?"

They all heard it; a tinkling of glass and a whining roar coming from the kitchen. The captain and Jenkins shot to their feet.

"It sounds as if Gregory's in trouble," said Sandy, getting up.

"They're climbing through the kitchen window!" cried Josh. He listened dumbstruck to the enraged roar of a tiger mingled with barked commands and the thump of bodies landing on the kitchen floor.

"Don't move from this room until I give the all-clear," the captain commanded. He and Jenkins raced downstairs. Josh heard shots and the agonised roar of a desperate tiger, followed by shouts and screams of terror. Then, he heard one last shot and the roaring ceased. He looked at Megs. Her hands were clenched, and her eyes had filled with tears. Sandy stood at the door. Without waiting to be asked, they all descended to the kitchen.

Two bodies lay tossed face downwards on the floor. The captain had made some effort to clear up the mess, pushing the chairs and table to one end of the room and covering the upper parts of the bodies with blankets, but enough blood spattered the ceiling and window-panes to suggest what an enraged tiger could do. Most of the chairs were broken and shards of glass lay scattered around the room.

Sandy sat quietly sobbing by the fireside, hunched over the still carcass of the tiger.

"There are two more pirates outside," said the captain. He moved along on his hands and knees sweeping up fragments of glass. "I think I shot one of them. Jenkins has gone after the other. We should never have left this place unguarded. Not even for an hour. Let that be a lesson to us."

"Gregory's dead," wailed Megs. "He was the sweetest tiger in the world. He never hurt anyone."

"He didn't do a bad job with those two intruders," commented the captain, getting up and giving the tiger an unsympathetic prod with the toe of his boot. "Anyway, he's not dead. I don't see any bullet holes." He pulled a dart from the tiger's haunches. "That was the noise you first heard. They shot him through the window with a stun gun. They must have been watching the house all day. They knew all about the tiger in the kitchen and planned to put him out of action. Luckily for us they didn't leave time for the drug to take effect. When they came into the room, he got a bit annoyed; to put it mildly," he added, looking round the room.

"But we heard shots!" exclaimed Josh.

"It's quite hard to shoot an animal at close range when he's in full spring. If you ask me, I wouldn't waste your pity on a healthy tiger."

As he spoke, Gregory began to stir, and Sandy's face flushed with joy.

CHAPTER SEVEN

The journey to Discovery Island took less than two hours but they were stuck for three rainy days in Greystones, the town harbour. Three days of adult supervision, with nothing to do! Josh felt his quest for the stone slipping out of reach

He found Megs on deck, wrapped in a blanket and sitting on a coil of old rope under a canvas awning. Gregory snoozed at her side, wheezing and hiccupping in his sleep.

"Hi, Megs. What are you doing on deck?"

"Looking out for the raven. Someone's got to."

"Yea, I suppose."

"What have you been doing, you and Sandy? It's eleven o'clock."

"I dunno," he said, running his hand through his hair and trying to remember. "Chatting, playing cards, having breakfast. Yea, have you seen the breakfast? The food's fantastic. How come you never eat there?"

Megs snorted. "Because when I get up – at the normal time, when it's still morning – to make sure Gregory gets fed and keep a look-out for the raven, I have to share the breakfast table with Tufton Pims. No thanks."

"What do you talk about?"

"Himself, mainly, and his success at just about everything. He's a young man in a hurry. That's what he told me."

"Young? He's already lost most of his hair; and his chin too, come to think of it."

Megs grinned. Then she looked round as if to make sure nobody was listening. "Seriously, Josh," she said, "isn't that the first thing you'd do, if you were the Prince and you wanted the stone that much – plant spies on this boat?"

"Tufton? Yes, we've got to watch out for him. There may be others we don't know about too; members of the crew, perhaps. That's the problem with this voyage," said Josh. "It's safe from attack because of the ceremonial bit, and it's free, and we've got protection…but it's got its own risks." He shook his head in confusion.

"You mean the Prince – whoever he is – can keep tabs on us and pick us off whenever he wants," said Megs.

"Exactly," said Josh, turning to her in excitement. "And it's nice to have an armed guard but it stops us from getting things done."

"It stops you, you mean," said Megs. She shook off her blanket and stood up. "Have you noticed something? The sun's come out." She stooped and tore off a hunk of bread from a loaf she'd stored in a paper bag, scattering a few crumbs on the table in front of her.

Josh stood and watched. "What are you doing?"

Megs threw up her hands. "Honestly, Josh. What does it look like? Have you forgotten why we're here? I'm trying to attract the raven."

"With a few crumbs? Why not a whole loaf?"

"Because he'd just seize it and fly off. We want to tempt him to stay, remember?"

"But will he see the crumbs from up there?"

"Ravens can see for miles." Megs went over and filled a bowl with milk which she placed beside the crumbs. She turned back to Josh. "If you want to make yourself useful, take those binoculars and look over in that direction. You see the cliff over to the left of the harbour. That's where his nest is supposed to be, according to Surly. I'll go and prepare Gregory."

Josh nodded. They both knew that Gregory needed to be coaxed into wakefulness before his roars could frighten away the raven.

"Have you seen anything yet?" Megs whispered. She knelt in front of the tiger, gently stroking him beneath the ears.

Josh struggled to focus on the right spot. "Aren't you being a bit optimistic?"

"After three days of rain!" Megs exclaimed. "The poor bird will be starving."

The tiger began to stir. He opened one eye and raised his huge jaws to sniff the wind. Megs placed a hand over his nose. "Hush, Gregory," she whispered. "The raven's on its way. Any moment now!"

"I think I've seen something," Josh announced. Suddenly he felt wide awake and conscious of his quest. "It may be nothing. Just a black speck." He put down his binoculars and scanned the sky with his naked eyes. "Yes, I can just see it."

"Is it moving?"

"Wait, I've lost it. No, it's over there. It's grown bigger – more like a black rag."

The black rag became two beating wings. "It's him!" he cried. "It's definitely a bird!"

The raven loomed into view, circling overhead, making a few darting swoops towards the breadcrumbs on the table in front of them and then veering away, tossed and buffeted by the wind.

"He's seen the food," whispered Megs. "Do you think our presence will scare him away?"

"I wouldn't imagine so," observed Gregory, with watchful eyes. "Smash and grab, that's the way with ravens, even elderly ravens like Crackjaw. You can be sure he's seen us, even from that distance. He probably even knows who I am. He'll land on the table, any moment now – you mark my words – and make his getaway as soon as he's got what he wants."

"I've got the rest of the loaf, here, under my jersey," whispered Megs. "I thought I could show it, to tempt him a bit closer. Do you think, if we offer him the loaf, he will be willing to help us?"

Gregory pondered this question, observing the raven's circular approach out of the corner of one eye. "Helpfulness. Hm. Let's say that he's had four hundred years in which to develop that admirable quality and I fear it may have eluded him."

"So you're saying he won't help us," asked Josh in disbelief.

"Not unless I threaten to eat him."

"Sh! He's coming our way," cried Megs.

Just then, the raven stopped circling and dropped out of the sky, swooping down to settle with a great flapping of wings on the table.

They kept still, waiting for the bird to get used to their presence and peck up the scattered crumbs.

"Hi," said Megs, keeping her voice level, "You must be Crackjaw."

"I could be," he squawked, with beak to the side, one beady eye peering across at her.

"Would you like some more food?"

"I wouldn't say no," he croaked. "How come you understand my language?"

"I'm Megs," she said brightly. "And this is Josh. As a matter of fact, he's the pirate Guardian."

"I don't hold with Guardians. Anyway, stop telling porkies. I know who he is, and I know who you are. You're just a girl."

"Have it your way," said Megs. "I'm just a girl offering you food. If you don't make a move, I'll give it to Gregory."

With a sudden dive, Crackjaw settled on the deck beside the awning. Megs smiled at him and broke off a piece of the loaf. At the same moment, Gregory, who had appeared to be sleeping up to now, shot out a paw and pinned him to the deck.

"Sorry, about that, Crackjaw," he murmured. "Don't try to peck me, or I might do you serious damage with my other paw. We don't want to do that, do we? We want to feed you. But first, we want you to answer a simple question."

The raven's ragged feathers shot in all directions. "What's all this 'we' business? 'We don't want this. We don't want that.' I don't see any 'we'. I'm not telling you anything! I've been tricked!"

"I wouldn't call it a trick," murmured Gregory. "We just want to pick your brains for a moment. Mm! It does smell delicious, that food. I think after all I might be tempted to eat it myself."

"It's only bread," countered the raven. "You can't fool me! Tigers aren't interested in bread."

"When we're really hungry," admitted the tiger. "We eat anything. Even a scrawny old raven would go down a treat. Mm!"

"There's no need to be rude," croaked Crackjaw, shuddering. "What's your question?"

"Grimshaw!" said Megs, "Do you remember a couple who fled to this island a very long time ago?"

"Why do you want to know?"

"Have some more bread," said Megs.

The raven soon had his beak full. Finally, he tipped back his head, made a curious wriggling movement with his neck as he swallowed the food, eyed the remainder of the loaf that she still held in her hand and decided to be helpful. "I do remember a couple called Grimshaw," he croaked.

"Was one of them, the woman perhaps, wearing an onyx stone round her neck on a golden chain?"

"How did you know that?" squawked Crackjaw, fluffing out his feathers.

"You tried to steal it from her," purred Gregory. "Ravens like you adore pretty stones."

"I'm not a thief!" protested the raven, hopping up and down with rage and making stabs at the tiger's paw. "Who says I'm a thief?"

"Of course, you're not a thief," said Josh, wishing he could smooth his aged feathers without risking a finger "We just want to know what she did with that stone."

"How should I know? She shooed me away with her broomstick!"

"Thank you, Crackjaw, you've been such a help," purred the tiger, releasing his grip. "Now, perhaps you would like to join us for some food?"

The raven stretched his wings and turned his beak this way and that, sizing up his options. Then, without warning, he approached the loaf which Megs had just released from her hand, speared it with his beak and took off in a lopsided flight towards his distant nest.

Josh heard the sound of voices behind him and turned to see Sandy approaching, deep in conversation with Jenkins and the captain, Jack Ketch.

"Hi. We've just been talking to Crackjaw," said Meg, as if it was no big deal.

"Crackjaw. Oh, the raven!" exclaimed the captain, walking towards them in his usual brisk fashion.

"The Grimshaws definitely had the stone. The wife took it."

"Then there's nothing to delay us from making a trip to the island and paying a call on this Forbes fellow, said the captain, taking a seat at the table and pulling up another chair for Jenkins. "But we'll have to be careful. Have you heard the news? A bomb went off yesterday. Fleck's been busy, it seems."

"You mean another circlet?" asked Josh. Instant suspicions tumbled through his mind.

"I'm afraid so."

"Do you think they got Forbes?"

The captain's unblinking, blue eyes urged him to continue.

"I mean it's like what they did with Sedgeworth."

"It could have been Forbes," said the captain. "Let's hope not. The police are not releasing details."

"Why does Fleck want these stones, anyway?" asked Megs.

Josh turned to her. He thought he knew the answer to this one. "Money," he said. "The Prince must be paying him. And mischief too, probably. He gets his kicks out of showing that he's cleverer than anyone else."

The captain nodded. "Yes, that sounds like Fleck. Take a seat, everyone. We haven't got long. We'd better go and check out this Forbes fellow soon – assuming he's still alive."

"The boat's not back yet," complained Jenkins. "Tufton borrowed it this morning and hasn't returned yet."

"That's the last time he plays that trick on us," said the captain, "We'll have to wait. In the meantime, my young friend has a little trick to show you. It may save one of our lives one day so watch carefully. Come on, Sandy."

Sandy had been waiting patiently for this moment. He held up the brass circlet for inspection. "I've been looking at the circuitry," he explained. "There are four coloured balls inserted into the circlet. Well, you can't see one of them because that's the bomb, but you can see the yellow one with the maker's logo – the Fleck – and the red and blue ones. I was up half the night trying to unlock it. And then I thought of something."

"The moment of truth," suggested the captain.

Sandy looked puzzled but decided to plod on. "We know that the yellow ball in not even connected to the circuit and the green ball brings death, so I decided to concentrate on the blue and red balls instead."

"Pleasure and pain?" asked Megs, holding up a hand like a model pupil.

"Yes, except that I started to wonder how you could transmit pleasure through an electric charge. It's obvious really. Pain is an electric shock. But pleasure? It's just the absence of pain. In other words, the electricity is switched off. So that's when I decided to take a closer look at the blue ball which doesn't seem to be doing anything. See for yourself. Do you notice anything?

"What are we looking for?" asked Jenkins, picking up the circlet in his huge hands and inspecting the blue ball. He shrugged and passed the circlet to Josh.

Josh gave it a blank stare. "I can't see anything special about it," he admitted.

"Would this help?" asked Sandy, handing him a tiny screwdriver.

Megs leant over Josh's shoulder. "I've got it!" she cried. "It has a tiny circle at the top. It's hard to see because it's been painted blue like the rest of the ball; only a shade lighter. None of the other balls have that!"

Josh applied the screwdriver to the blue circle. A minute piece of metal came away from the ball and stuck to the magnetic tip of the screwdriver. "It's not a circle at all!" exclaimed Josh. "It's a screw head!"

"That's right," said Sandy proudly. "All you have to do is remove the screw and the connection is broken. But you need a small screwdriver, and it must be magnetic. Now try this." He carefully replaced the screw and held the screwdriver some distance away from the circlet. "I don't think Fleck could be bothered with getting up close," he said. "I expect he just did this."

He pressed the top of the screwdriver with his finger and pointed it at the circlet. Instantly the tiny screw revolved at speed and flew out of the ball.

Megs raised a warning hand. "Put it away!" she hissed. Too late; Tufton Pims had emerged from the hatchway behind them. He sported a light blue suit and a bright red tie. His broad, square face creased in a satisfied smile. "I say! Circlets and bombs! One of Fleck's circs, as they say in the trade. Who's been a naughty boy then? Mind if I join you?"

"I'm afraid we were just leaving," said the captain. "As a matter of fact, we were waiting for the dinghy to return so that we could go on shore." He was still mulling over Tufton's comments. "'Fleck's circs', eh? Is that what they call them?" he said. "You must have come across quite a few on your business trips. What took you so long, by the way?"

Josh thought he detected a nervous flicker in Tufton's eyes. He seemed in a hurry to get away. "Had things to do," he said.

The captain gave him a hard stare. "If you play that trick on us again," he said, "I will personally throw you off the boat. I hope I have made myself clear."

"Sorry about that," said Tufton, in a blustering effort to maintain his dignity. "Well, I see you chaps are eager to get off." He looked at his watch and added, "And I've got some phone calls to make," he said. Must press on."

"That man spells trouble," warned the captain. "I suspect he is dancing to someone else's tune, and that tune isn't leading us to Amaryllis. I'm taking Josh on shore in a moment to meet Forbes. Anyone else want to come?"

"I'll stay here, if you don't mind," said Sandy, not getting up. "I don't feel comfortable leaving Gregory on his own."

"Not with Tufton around," agreed Megs. "I'm staying here with Sandy."

CHAPTER EIGHT

After parting with Jenkins at the harbour, the captain led Josh through a cobbled maze of streets on the hilly outskirts of town. "This is the old part," he said. "He lives round here somewhere; up that street opposite, I think."

As they climbed the steeply winding street, past endless timber-framed houses bent with age, they became aware of a ghostly figure swaying towards them. John Bosworthy's shirt was torn and stained, and his face looked pale and unshaven. He seemed to be walking in a dream.

"I say. The captain, isn't it, and Josh? I am so glad to see you again. I think that…Dash me, I don't know what I think! I was going to say something. The thought came to me a moment ago and now it's gone again." He leaned forward and tried to snatch it out of the air with one bony hand. "No, it's gone for good, I'm afraid."

He swayed and nearly toppled over, but the captain stepped in to hold him up with two strong arms. "You're in a bad way, Bosworthy. What have you been doing?"

John Bosworthy fixed two mournful eyes on the captain's face. "That's the point, you see," he said. "I can't remember where I've been. Pufton – or is it Tufton? – showed me the way, I think. That's how I must have got here. Then I found these men. I don't know how I met them exactly. I must have been walking along the street. And the next thing I remember I was in a bar. A bit like that bar on the corner. It could have been that bar."

"Tell us more about the men, Bosworthy."

"Three of them, I think. Maybe more. I couldn't see exactly. It was very dark and smoky in the room. I remember lots of laughter, and it all seemed to be quite friendly at first. Yes. Then suddenly it turned nasty.! 'He's a spy!' That's what I heard one of them say. He said. 'He's a spy!' I don't know why he said that. Did I tell you what he said?"

"You told us, Bosworthy. Now, think very hard. What did they do to you? Did they make you drink something?"

"They tied me to a chair. I remember that."

"Do you remember why they thought you were a spy? Were you asking questions about the Prince, for example?"

"The Prince! That's it! 'Perhaps he'd like to meet him, since he's so interested!' I remember that bit. That's about all I remember. I think they took turns, after that, asking me questions and then hitting me."

"What sort of questions?" asked Josh curiously.

"Why, it's Josh, isn't it? Did I remember to say hello to you?"

"You said hello. What sort of questions did these men ask you?"

"Now I come to think of it, questions about you mainly, where you were going, what you were looking for. It was no use. I couldn't remember. One moment–"

He lurched sideways and vomited on the edge of the cobbled street.

"Excuse me." He stood upright again, flopping around like a rag doll with the captain's arm round his waist.

At that moment Josh saw a bent figure heading in their direction.

"Hello, am I right in thinking that you are Josh Flagsmith?" called an elderly voice from the other side of the street. A gnome-like person with prominent ears, dressed in a well-used check jacket, hurried across the street to greet them. "Excuse me, you must be Josh Flagsmith. And this, I believe, is Captain Ketch. The other gentleman, I am afraid, is not familiar to me."

"How did you know my name?" asked Josh.

At this point, they had reached the bar on the corner, which turned out to be called 'The Pirates Rest'. Their new acquaintance pointed to a picture of Josh fixed to a billboard on the wall of the bar. 'Wanted. Josh Flagsmith. Any information leading to his discovery will be handsomely rewarded. Enquire within.'

Josh scrutinised the picture of himself, which had to be at least a year old, and peered into the dark interior of the pub, dreading what shadows lurked inside.

"I am not seeking a reward, you will no doubt be relieved to hear," the stranger was explaining. "I am, in fact, Frederic Forbes, and I have been expecting you. My house is just here, so, please follow me. I can't tell you how much pleasure it gives me to meet the son of David Flagsmith. And the captain too, of course. And the…other young gentleman."

"John Bosworthy," explained the captain. "He's not himself at the moment, I'm afraid. He's just been set upon and plied with drink – probably in that bar on the corner."

Frederic Forbes looked up from the struggle with his front door key. "Indeed, indeed. Poor fellow. I can't say I'm surprised. I'm afraid my neighbourhood has gone downhill over the past few years. In fact, that bar is notorious for all kinds of criminal activity on this island. Let's go upstairs. It's rather dark inside, so mind how you walk."

He paused at the second floor. "A nasty incident occurred round here yesterday," he explained. "It's shaken me up a bit. You may have heard about it on the news?" He gave a little shiver and hurried up the last set of stairs. "Let's get that fellow…Bosworthy, did you say?"

"Yes, Bosworthy," said Josh.

"Oh dear me, yes, Bosworthy. Let's find him a bed in my apartment and I'll give him a little something to counteract the effects of the potion. I fancy myself as rather an expert on potions."

They arrived in a low ceilinged, oak-panelled room with mullioned windows overlooking the street and bookshelves covering most of the three remaining walls. Opposite the windows, another low door led to the rest of the apartment. The captain followed Frederic Forbes through this door and laid John Bosworthy out in the bedroom, while Frederic fussed around in the kitchen next door mixing up some herbal medicine.

Josh wandered back into the sitting room and stared at the bookshelves, listening to the enthusiastic patter in the background. "It's mostly milk," Frederic Forbes was explaining, "plus a few other ingredients with long, technical names. According to folklore, the lactic acid in milk counteracts the effect of *Oblivia Preciosa* - which I assume to be the liquid in question. If you would just raise his head a little for me, like so, I am going to spoon a little of this medicine into his mouth. He looks about ready to fall asleep now, so I think we can safely leave him there for a bit and, when he wakes up, he'll be a new man. You mark my words."

The gnome-like figure re-emerged into the room, still chattering like a man who'd been starved of conversation for weeks. "Now let's go and make ourselves comfy. I have prepared some light refreshments for you. I must say how very exciting this all is, to meet you and young Josh Flagsmith in the flesh. Please, do sit down. That's right. On the leather sofa. I'll take the old armchair opposite. Tea for everyone? And here's some sandwiches I have just prepared for you. Crab or cucumber. I hope you are comfortable with the choice. Good, so please help yourselves. Don't be shy. They all have to go."

Josh shifted in his seat under the warmth and intensity of the probing eyes, smiling at him and plying him with sandwiches.

"So, young man," said Frederic, pulling his chair closer. "I believe you have some questions for me. I have done my homework, as you can see." He pointed to the small round table beside his chair, where books and manuscripts were neatly strewn. Where shall we start?"

"Grimshaw," began Josh.

"Ah! You've got there already. Good lad. Only the name soon turned to Dagren. You see this? It's the diary of Hubert Dagren. You can hold it in your hands if you like. The cover is made of leather and the paper – or parchment – is nearly 365 years old. This is the page I want you to look at. Here, I'll read it for you. 'Today I toke into my house a yonge servinge wench by the name of Emily Grimshaw, the only dochter of one Greta Grimshaw who came to this island some ten yeres ago with her husbonde, one Robert Grimshaw, who was once in the service of Prince Rupert…'

Josh held the centuries old manuscript in his hands. Greta Grimshaw's daughter! His hands began to tingle as he turned the pages.

His host was still speaking. "It goes on for several pages, but the short and the long of it is that Greta Grimshaw lost her husband." He shot Josh a sly glance. "Well, it's my belief that she poisoned him in much the same way as she poisoned Rupert the Rotten. There was plenty of speculation about that in her own day. Anyway, as you can imagine, for an exiled widow with a dubious reputation, life was not going to be easy for Greta Grimshaw. So what does she do? She lives off her daughter! First finding her a job with a local landowner, then encouraging her to seize the main chance and marry him. It's all here if you can read between the lines."

"What happened to Emily Dagren?" asked Josh.

"Ah! Well, the diaries can't help us any further here because Hubert Dagren met with an unfortunate riding accident soon after the marriage was consummated – the work of Greta Grimshaw again – who knows? We do know from a separate source that Emily Dagren married again."

Frederic Forbes reached for the next heavy volume in his pile, the *Greystones Chronicle.*

"Here we are – 351 years ago – as it happens only two years after Hubert Dagren's death, the marriage is announced of one Duke Fraterno to 'the yonge and excedinge beautiful widow, Emily Dagren'. Now, fortunately for our purposes, this Duke Fraterno was quite an important figure in those days. His house still stands and is open to the public, if you are willing to pay the extortionate admission fees that they charge nowadays. Be that as it may, the most interesting room in the Duke's house is the portrait gallery, and here you are! This is a copy of the painting of Emily Fraterno as she then was, in the year 55 AD; that's after the disaster, which happened about 400 years ago. What do you notice, apart from the fact that she could hardly be described as beautiful?"

Josh stared in astonishment. "She's wearing Rupert's stone!"

"Exactly. Look, do have some more sandwiches. Captain, you're not interested in all this nonsense about a stone. You're a man of action. So do please tuck in."

The sandwiches, which had all been cut into small squares with their crusts removed, were piled high on the plate. The captain helped himself to a handful while pondering his reply. "Mr Forbes, my mission is to get this young man safely to Amaryllis," he said. "This business of the stone is of vital importance to the mission – either to find the damn thing or to make sure that nobody else finds it. You with me so far?"

"Indeed I am, Mr Ketch."

"Then am I right in thinking that you know more about this stone than anyone else in the world?"

"I suppose that's true in a way, Mr Ketch."

"Then there's only one thing for it, Mr Forbes. You'll have to come with us."

Josh saw a mixture of emotions flicker across the gnome-like face. Surprise. Modesty. Confusion. But he had the distinct impression that behind all this show of reluctance lay a twinkle in the eyes which suggested that he'd already worked this out.

"Otherwise, you'd be a dead man, see," the captain was explaining. "And we don't want that, do we?"

"Well, I certainly don't," agreed Frederic Forbes.

"Because they'd follow Josh's trail to the house – if they have not done so already – and they'd find you and squeeze you dry like a lemon. And then they'd kill you. So how long do you think it would take you to get yourself ready for such a voyage?"

"My bags are packed for just such an eventuality," replied Frederic Forbes, "and my daughter has consented to feed the cat in my absence."

"You too are a man of action, Mr Forbes."

Josh couldn't contain his impatience. "But we can't just leave the island like that," he murmured. "If the stone is still here, surely we have to track it down…somehow?"

"Ah, but it isn't," said the captain, smiling.

Josh stared at him in confusion. "How do you know?"

"I don't think our friend, Mr Forbes, would be in a hurry to leave if he thought the stone was still here."

 Frederic's smile said it all.

 "Besides," continued the captain. The name 'Fraterno' is a dead giveaway. He was a pirate, like his new wife, Emily Grimshaw. Around that time, the colonists held purges on Discovery Island. A man of property like Fraterno? He wouldn't wait to be shot down or led away for execution. He would have escaped, probably to Crown Colony, wouldn't he?"

"It's not a very common name, Fraterno," agreed Frederic Forbes, reaching out for quite a modern-looking catalogue. There you are, you see. This is a recent telephone directory of Crown Colony. There's only one Fraterno listed here. An interesting man. I've met him."

"You've met him? What did he say?" asked Josh.

"He wasn't the right Fraterno."

"Oh."

"But he did show me this, which I found very interesting. It's a family tree. The date we are interested in is 221 years ago. And there's the name again. Emily Fraterno."

"But that would make her nearly 150 years old!" protested Josh.

"Well, she's not the same Emily, of course, but she is a direct descendant. And she wasn't called Fraterno. She married a merchant seaman called Digby Fortune and they emigrated about 200 years ago with their baby daughter to Humphrey's Island. And that, more or less, is where the trail ends."

"On Humphrey's Island!" exclaimed Josh. He knew the island lay just on the Prince's doorstep.

"I have never been there, alas!" said Frederic Forbes, "but it is a very large island, I believe, and much of the interior is unexplored. The idea that it was named after an explorer called Humphrey is quite wrong. It actually owes its name to a humpless camel which the first colonists hunted to extinction. 'Hump-free' – get it? Anyway, I have found an interesting reference in the works of an anthropologist called Frank Gibson. Towards the end of the last century, he made a study of some of the primitive tribes living in the tropical rain forest of Humphrey's Island and, among the tribes he listed, was one called the Fortune tribe. Now I happen to know that there's a man in Crown Colony who recently led an expedition to the jungles of Humphrey's Island. He's none other than the famous explorer, Sir William Feathers. So that, I feel, should be our next endeavour – to speak to Sir William and, with the benefit of his advice, go to Humphrey's Island and seek our Fortune, as it were."

CHAPTER NINE

J osh found the captain and Jenkins leaning over the ship's railings staring through the morning haze at the capital of Crown Colony; looking at it now, he couldn't work out why the sight didn't fill him with wonder and excitement as it had on his first voyage.

The captain looked at his watch. "You're early this morning, Josh. I'm impressed! How's Bosworthy? Have you seen him?"

Josh laughed. "Yea, having breakfast; chatting about the medical trade and stuff. He didn't seem put off by what happened to him yesterday."

"Good. Come and see how far we've travelled overnight. You're looking at the centre of our little federation; first Colony Island, then Discovery and now Crown Colony. It's by far the biggest of the three."

"What's the name of this town? I don't remember it."

"Paradise City!" said Jenkins, dismissing the view with a disgusted wave of the hand. "Paradise City! Funny how they always think up nice names for horrible places. That's the hub of the federation, Crown Colony. It's where all the money is – at least if your name's Magnus Maxtrader."

Josh leant on the railings and saw a noisy, smoky harbour packed with trading vessels moored in numbered rows. The jetties were lined with cranes, leaning forward like giant storks to pluck their bundles out of the air. Dockers and tradesmen rushed up and down the piers, receiving and giving shouted commands. A few ramshackle offices and warehouses lined the wharves. Beyond, tall, white skyscrapers loomed like icebergs, lit with flickering advertisements, over the yachts and fishing dories tossing in the polluted waves.

"Why are we stopping there?" asked Sandy, emerging bleary-eyed from the hatchway.

"It's part of our ceremonial tour of duty," explained the captain. He looked at his watch again. "We're leaving the ship in an hour. Better tell Megs."

Megs waved when she saw them and raised her eyes in a gesture of mock despair. She lay with her back against the awning, idly stroking the tiger's neck and listening to his whining roar. "But you saved our lives!" she kept saying, "Single-handed. If it weren't for you, we would all be dead by now or wearing those horrible circlets round our necks. That makes you a hero."

"What's the matter?" whispered Sandy.

Josh came and sat beside him at the table next to the awning. "We're off to see an explorer called Feathers," he said. "He knows where we can find the stone."

"Oh, the stone," said Sandy. "I meant, what's the matter with Gregory?"

"Nothing," whispered Megs. "He's just feeling sorry for himself."

"Perhaps he's hungry?"

"Sh!"

"It makes me a murderer," persisted Gregory. "More than 400 years I have lived on this earth and never, since I was a young tiger, have I broken the vow that we animals of the talking kind made to Matilda never to attack or kill a human being."

"Well, I'm glad you did!" exclaimed Megs, giving the boys another wink." You were wonderful! So quick and brave! You saved us all."

The tiger lifted his great head. "Do you think so? Do you really think so? Well, I suppose my actions could be seen in a noble night but I'm still a murderer."

"You're still an actor," thought Josh.

Megs snorted. "Listen, Gregory," she cried. "You killed two people who were trying to kill you. Enough's enough. Now let's forget it!"

"How can I ever forget?"

She sighed. "Maybe food would help?"

"I don't really feel very hungry at the moment but I suppose I could force myself," he responded, sniffing the air with a wistful hint of anticipation.

Josh flinched as a raw steak sailed over his head and landed with a thump within an inch of Gregory's nose. Turning round, he saw Tufton Pims looming over the table, a bit glassy eyed and smelling of stale beer.

"Mind if I join you? Nice sunny day. Here you are. He upturned the contents of a plastic bag on the table. Snacks for everyone and something a bit special for the noble beast at your side."

Gregory got up and sniffed the meat.

Megs shot to her feet. "What's that? Steak? The tiger's already eaten, thank you," she said, snatching the meat from his grateful jaws. She ran to the ship's side and tossed it into the sea.

"You never know with tigers" said Sandy, groping for a tactful explanation. "Some of them are allergic to meat."

"Unless it's fat and walking around on two legs," said Megs, giving Sandy an angry stare.

Josh held his breath but Tufton seemed too drunk or thick-skinned to notice. He just grinned and settled his ample frame in a deck chair, on the opposite side of the table from the tiger.

Since nobody volunteered to speak, he began to sing a little song to himself under his breath:

"Oh, I'm a travelling salesman and I sail the seven seas

With my credit card, and smart phone and laptop on my knees

"Oh, I'm a travelling salesman and I do my best to please

"With...."

He looked up. "I can't remember the next bit," he said. "Anyway, I'm glad I've found you all here together," he continued. "Look, you can call me Tuffers. That's how I'm known to my friends."

"Tell us about your friends, Tuffers," said Megs, in a voice loaded with sarcasm. "Do they come from Windfree?"

"Windfree? No! All over the place!" He leant back and belched. "'Scuse me! Matter of fact, one of my friends is a local chappie, a journalist. He has shown a great interest in your story. Three kids on the search for a missing stone."

Megs shrugged. "I haven't lost a stone. Have you, Josh? If anything, I'd say you'd gained one." She flashed her dark eyes at Josh and Sandy like warning beacons.

Tufton shook his head and tried another tack. "A shame about that business with the Cat Lady!" he exclaimed, winking at Megs. "And all because of a wretched stone. One almost wonders if things would have turned out differently if you had just given her what she wanted. The stone I mean. You do still have it, don't you?" he asked, turning to Josh.

Josh gave him a blank stare. "Why do you want to know?" he asked in as neutral a voice as he could manage.

Tufton grinned. "It's not me that's interested. It's my journalist friend. The paper he works for would pay good money for a 'human interest' story like that. And then there's this mention of another stone which once belonged to Prince Rupert. You haven't found it, have you?"

Josh got up.

There was an awkward silence. Josh looked through him. "We haven't been looking for it, have we Sandy?" he said.

"What? No. No we haven't." Sandy studied the progress of a fly across the table.

"Look, we're just about to go on shore," said Josh.

Tufton got up too and tapped him on the shoulder as he headed for the hatchway. "You want to know the good news?" he asked, turning his head and laughing. "I'm coming with you. Yes, I thought that would cheer you up!"

"What was all that about?" asked Sandy, staring at his broad, departing back. "Why did you throw away a perfectly good steak?"

"How did I know it wasn't poisoned?" asked Megs.

"Do you think it was poisoned?" Sandy asked.

"No," said Megs.

Josh smiled. You couldn't win an argument with Megs. Normal rules didn't apply.

"Otherwise," she went on, "I'd have shoved it down his throat. I just think he's up to no good, and I didn't like all that probing about Josh's stone."

"Yes, but that came after," Sandy persisted. "First he gave him the steak-"

"And then you explained that some tigers are vegetarian," Josh cut in. "That was a master stroke. Look! I think we have another visitor."

Josh had his eyes on the hatchway where a small, elderly man in an old pair of jeans and an open-neck shirt was poised on the top step and peering short-sightedly in their direction. He beamed when he saw Josh and hurried forward at a hunched angle to greet him.

"Frederic Forbes," whispered Josh, "the historian."

He seized Josh's hand and shook it vigorously, "Hello again, Josh. And you must be Sandy. And Megs. I have heard so much about you. And this...this must be...the tiger." He stooped in front of Gregory and rubbed his hands. "I must admit I have never seen a tiger before, not even in a – well, never mind this is a completely different animal. A tiger of the talking kind, I understand. And he has a name. Gregory, I have been told. Tell me, Megs, do you think he would mind if I stroked him? I don't wish to seem patronising. It's just that. Well, you know, I have never touched such a handsome animal before."

Megs smiled and offered him a seat at the table. "He can understand you even if you can't understand him," she said. "That's the way it is with talking animals. And I can tell you he feasts on compliments. Look, he's greeting you."

Frederic threw his arms around the tiger whose face nuzzled into his chest, emitting a purring noise like a throbbing motor.

The captain strode towards them, accompanied by Jenkins. "Right. Let's go!" he exclaimed, pointing towards the ship's ladder. Twenty feet below, a motor launch tossed in the water, waiting to take them the short distance to the quay. "Are you joining us, Forbes?"

The old man smiled and shook his head. "I think I'll duck out of this one if you don't mind," he said. "Crown Colony has never been one of my favourite places. Besides, I have so much to discuss with my friend, John Bosworthy."

"Where are we meeting Feathers?" asked Megs.

"We're going to a hostelry called 'The Angel's Arms'," said the captain.

"Won't it be full of people?" asked Josh.

"Good question. No, it's empty. Up for sale. That's why Sir William selected it as a safe place to meet."

The captain had put one foot on the ladder when Tufton Pims appeared.

Josh shrugged. Tufton had a brown leather suitcase and looked even more pleased with himself than usual. "I thought I'd join you, if you don't mind," he said with a chuckle. "I've got some business of my own to transact in this fair city."

Josh saw the look of resignation on the captain's face as he let him tag along.

CHAPTER TEN

The motor launch with Jenkins at the helm wove its way around the ships and smaller trading vessels moored on either side and stopped opposite the Customs Office. The captain and Jenkins jumped out and helped them all to disembark.

Just then Tufton barged past them and ran ahead into the building.

"What's he up to?" asked Jenkins.

Josh thought he saw a flicker of doubt in the captain's eyes. He blinked and came to a decision. "Too late to worry about that now," he said. "Let's go ahead with our plan."

They entered a vast, empty hall. Tufton stood at the far end talking with two officials. He turned and waved, then hurried through the exit at the far end of the hall.

"I don't like the look of this," whispered Jenkins. "I don't know what Tufton said to them, but he wasn't just passing the time of day."

A side door opened, and twelve customs officers stepped in and lined the wall facing them. Jenkins started to hum a little tune to himself. "Looks like trouble," he said. At that moment, the chief officer entered, brisk, bright and smiling, followed by two armed officers with sniffer dogs. He looked them up and down, referring to his notes. "Josh? Anyone here called Josh?"

Josh waved an uncertain arm.

"Right, Josh. You can go. Megs?"

Megs frowned. "What do you want?"

"You can go. Sandy? You're Sandy? You can go."

None of them moved.

The chief officer walked over to them. "You heard what I said. You kids are all free to go."

Megs shrugged at the two boys and they all looked at the captain.

"They're with us!" he protested. "I'm responsible for them."

"You, my friend," explained the chief officer, looking him up and down, "are responsible for a lot of things, it seems. Leave your baggage where it is and stand over there. That goes for your colleague too. Not you, Josh! You and your two friends are free to go. So, do what I say. I want you out of here."

Josh threw a questioning glance at the captain who replied. "There's nothing for it, Josh. Go ahead with the plan. We'll join you when we can - if not at The Angel's Arms, then later."

"The Angel's Arms?" the chief officer. "We'd better search that place too."

"Good, you do that," said the captain. "If anything happens to them while I'm being detained, you will have a lot to answer for."

The chief officer just nodded to two of his customs officers who stepped forward and grabbed Josh and Sandy by the arm, letting Megs follow them out of the building.

Josh led the way onto the pavement of a busy three-lane highway leading into the centre of town. He thought about Fleck's last words. He must have been waiting for this moment. Any one of the suited pedestrians striding to work could be one of his agents, waiting to grab his stone and pump him for information about William Feathers and the Fortune family and the stone of love. He felt scared and wary, and disappointed at the loss of the captain and Jenkins, but above all he felt a rush of excitement at being alone in a big city and on the verge of tracking down that stone.

"When do you think they'll release them?" asked Megs, hurrying along at his shoulder.

"They'll probably miss our next sailing," Sandy called out. "My dad says customs officers can hold you for weeks, even if you're innocent."

"Then they'll have to join us later," said Josh. He slowed his pace to avoid getting swept away from his friends by the impatient jostling crowd, most of them wearing suits and holding mobile phones to their ears as they hurried to get to work on time. "Let's get out of this." He shouted. "There's a café coming up on our left. We need to stop and think."

They hurried down some steps into a dimly lit café and stood for a moment by the doorway, adjusting to the silence. The regular clientele had all had breakfast and left for work. About twenty square tables laden with dirty cups and plates covered most of the area. An elderly gentleman in an overcoat sat in a far corner, watching a sullen, young waitress attending to the remains of fifty recent breakfasts. "Tell me, Miss!"

The waitress hardly looked up from the table she was clearing. "What is it this time?" she said with a sigh.

"Do you use that cloth for cleaning the dirty tables or for dirtying the clean ones?"

"Don't you be so cheeky, or you won't get served!"

The waitress saw them and pointed to a table facing the street. "You can take that one," she said, returning her weary attention to the table. "I'll attend to you in a moment."

"He must have put something in the captain's case," whispered Josh, taking a seat and waiting for his friends to join him. "That's why he was laughing to himself."

Sandy nodded. "I bet he's in league with whoever's behind this."

Josh gave him a playful punch. "He's in league with whoever's behind this," he repeated. "Inspector Sandy Oldways at his last press conference was willing to bet that the criminal was in league with other criminals who were behind this affair…."

Megs turned on him. "Stop it, Josh!"

"Stop what, Megs?"

"Stop teasing him."

Josh laughed. "That's what guys do, Megs," he explained. "We like teasing. Sandy doesn't mind, do you Sandy?"

"I wasn't listening," admitted Sandy. "Sorry, Megs." He blushed.

Megs raised her eyes to the ceiling. "Honestly, Sandy, you should learn to stick up for yourself." She turned to Josh. "These people want to get us on our own, especially you, so that they can get hold of that stone."

"I've been thinking," said Sandy. "Surely the neat thing would be to seize our boat and kidnap us at the same time. That way they could accompany us to Humphrey's Island and use our knowledge to obtain the stone of love. Maybe he really did put poison in that meat."

"Why on earth would he want to poison a tiger?" asked Josh.

"It's obvious," said Megs. "To make it easier to capture the boat."

"But Old Surly and his crew look as if they can defend themselves."

"They left before we did," said Megs. "I saw them go." She gasped as she realised what that meant. "Poor Gregory!" she cried. "We have to get back to that boat and save him!"

Josh nodded. "Let's hope Tuffer's friends haven't boarded her yet," he said, hurrying towards the exit. "Don't worry about us!" he called out to the waitress, "We're leaving!"

"Look at the crowd," he whispered, as they stepped out onto the pavement. He'd expected the morning rush hour to be over, but the street seemed even busier than before. This time, instead of hurrying towards the centre of town, the crowd streamed in a headlong rush towards the quay. Amid a buzz of nervous excitement, the word on everyone's lips was 'tiger'!

"Something's happened to Gregory!" he cried, pushing his way forward, followed by Sandy and Megs. Several faces in the crowd turned to protest but he plunged on regardless, shouting "This is an emergency! Our tiger's in danger!" Several voices in the crowd exclaimed, 'It's their tiger!' and the mood changed from hostility to immediate understanding, with the people in front jostling and pushing one another to the side as if to make way for an ambulance. The people who fell over themselves to get out of the way fastest were the ones who thought they were making way for the tiger itself.

On the quayside, an excited crowd observed the huge striped head bobbing up and down in the murky water.

"He's swimming!" exclaimed Sandy.

Megs looked unimpressed. "Yes. And showing off – but he'll have to watch out."

Josh found himself being pushed and jostled by more people crowding in to watch the spectacle. Some carried their children above their heads. "There he is!" they cried. "Isn't he magnificent? Where's he gone? Look, he's diving! Watch out! He's heading our way!"

"Thank goodness somebody's got sense," said Megs. "Look! Old Surly's arrived."

"Why? What can he do?" asked Sandy

"Stop Gregory getting shot."

Sandy's mouth hung open. "They wouldn't do that, would they?"

Megs stared at him in disbelief. "Of course they would, if they thought he was dangerous! These people have never seen a talking tiger before."

"Look! Surly's got the whole crew with him," said Sandy. "At least he'll be able to transport us back to the ship."

"What if Tufton's already captured it?" asked Megs.

"We'll just have to capture it back!" exclaimed Josh. "He's not going anywhere – not without my stone."

"And what about the captain and Jenkins?" asked Megs. "We can't just leave them!"

Josh thought about the situation for a second and said, "There's nothing we can do. They can join us later if need be."

"What's Surly doing?" asked Sandy. "He's got his arms round Gregory."

"He wants the crowd to see that he's not dangerous." Josh explained. "Listen!" He could hear a spreading murmur from the crowd.

"He's a talking tiger! He's from Amaryllis."

"Do you see that van? I think he's attracted the local press!"

Josh laughed, in spite of himself. Gregory was old and smart enough to have worked that bit out for himself.

Old Surly looked more grumpy than usual. He held a microphone which had just been shoved into his hand by a young lady who had managed to push her way through the group of journalists. "I'm from the *Crown Gazette,*" she was saying. "I would like to have a few words with this elegant tiger."

"His name's Gregory," said Old Surly.

"Yes, yes. Of course." She grabbed the microphone back and waved it in front of the tiger's nose. "Tell me, Gregory, what are your first impressions of Crown Colony?"

Josh smiled. Gregory had never been to Crown Colony but that wouldn't faze him. He simply opened his huge jaws and purred his pleasure at length, dwelling on the excellent shopping amenities, the modern architecture, the low crime rate, the booming economy, the wise government, the lack of prejudice against tigers.

"What a con artist!" Megs whispered in Josh's ear.

"He says he likes it," Old Surly explained, "He will recommend it to his children."

Gregory opened his jaws and gave a whining growl of protest.

"Does he have many children? Where do they live? How old are they?" cried the onlookers.

"He has two sons and the younger one is 370 years old," interpreted Old Surly.

"370. That can't be right! How old does that make him? Is he talking in tiger years or human years?"

"Talking animals," explained Old Surly, "live a very long time. Gregory himself is 403 years old. And that's in human years. If you ask me, that's quite old, even for a talking tiger."

"I'm a very old, very sad tiger," said Gregory, hanging his head in an old and sad-looking way, while Old Surly explained his remarks to the audience.

"Oh dear! Poor thing! Can we take a picture of him looking sad?"

"What's he doing now?" asked Sandy.

"Same as usual. Showing off," explained Megs. "Still, I'm glad he's not on the ship."

"At least he's safe," agreed Sandy, "and the crew are with him, so we've got nothing to fear."

Megs went over to Josh. "What's the matter?" she asked. "You've gone quiet."

"I was thinking."

"Go on."

The crowd on the quayside had started to thin out. Only a few stragglers remained to watch Gregory making his slow progress back through the water in the direction of the ship.

"Did Tufton know we were going to The Angel's Arms?" Josh asked.

Megs frowned. "I think we all knew."

Josh turned to her. "So that's it. Don't you see? They got us on our own so they could kidnap us or–"

Sandy finished the sentence for him. "Feathers! Isn't he the bloke that knows where the Prince's stone is hidden? So why not catch Feathers and then wait for you to turn up too?"

"What does your stone tell you?" asked Megs.

Josh felt a sharp pain between his eyes. He closed his fingers tightly round the stone in his pocket and the pain slowly vanished. He withdrew the stone from his pocket and watched it open to reveal an old bearded man tied to a chair, wearing one of Fleck's circlets.

"I might have guessed," muttered Josh. "Fleck's already there. He's fixed Feathers up with one of those circlets. We've got to rescue him!"

"But what about Surly?" asked Megs. "We've got to tell someone where we are!"

Josh felt the familiar rush of excitement as he worked it all out. "You're right, Megs. We'll have to split up. I'll deal with Fleck. You two tell Surly what's going on."

"'I'll deal with Fleck!" Megs mimicked him. She turned to face him in a sudden rage. "You're crazy! Deal with Fleck! Have you taken leave of your senses?"

Josh laughed. He fished a mobile phone from his pocket. "Hello, I want to report an emergency. The Angel's Arms. Yes. There's a man inside with a bomb attached to his neck. Ronald Fleck's with him. If you move fast, you can catch him. Sorry. No time for further questions. I'll meet you there in five minutes. My name's Smith. Josh Smith. Yes."

Josh couldn't hide his sense of triumph. "I don't know if they believed me, but they have got to act on the information, all the same. All I have to do is hail a taxi and stroll down to The Angel's Arms. I can leave the rest to the police."

Megs was crying now, fury mixing with her tears. She tugged him by the arm. "You're mad, Josh. You can't do this on your own!"

"No time, Megs," he shouted, pulling away from her. "Listen! You've got to explain everything to Surly. Tell him where I've gone." A sudden doubt struck him. "And stop off at the police station," he added. "Take Surly with you. Make sure they come to my rescue."

He dashed off to find a taxi before his two friends could stop him.

CHAPTER ELEVEN

Josh gripped his stone so tightly that his fingers ached as he sat in the back of the taxi heading for The Angel's Arms, knowing he had to get there before the police but not knowing if the police would come. If he didn't rescue Feathers soon, Fleck would squeeze the truth out of him, and the Prince would end up with that stone. Two stones! Fleck could easily seize the stone he carried in his pocket. Josh couldn't let him take that stone. He couldn't live without it. But he needed it with him now more than ever. He'd 'deal with Fleck'. With what? How? His heart beat so fast he couldn't think. He saw a blur of crowded streets and a deserted playground on the scruffy outskirts of town and heard a scrunch of wheels on gravel as the taxi drew up outside The Angel's Arms.

Josh tested the door and, finding it open, waited inside. He heard the roar of the taxi racing off. He hung in the cavernous space beside the open doorway, where he could see if the police arrived and hear any sound from the room above. He looked up at the high ceiling and heard nothing – not even a muffled murmur. A good sign. Or did it mean Feathers was dead? The dusty, stale air in the empty stairwell smelt of Fleck. He imagined his small, inhuman face looking down on him.

He looked at his watch. Ten minutes since he'd phoned the police – they had to come soon. Still no sound from above – what was happening up there? Did Fleck expect him to come? Of course! He'd be ready for him. With a knife? With a gun? With Osborne and his bag of tricks? Josh took a deep breath to stop his legs from shaking. He looked through the open door at the empty street, then up the dark stairway to the landing and the shadow on the right of the landing which led up more stairs to the room above. If he didn't mount the stairs soon, he'd never do it.

The police hadn't arrived. Too bad! He placed one shaky foot on the first step. As soon as he transferred his full weight to it, he heard a creak. He froze and looked up, his breath coming in quick pants. No sound from above. Noiselessly, he tried the next step and the next, looking back at the open doorway and willing the police to arrive.

In a few more steps, he reached the landing where the steps turned at right angles towards the upper floor. He looked up. Above, on the top landing, the door on his left stood open; Fleck must be somewhere behind that door. He put his foot on the next step. No turning back now.

He fingered his stone again. Just holding it gave him confidence; he knew he could walk through that door – he didn't have a better choice. He took off his shoes and padded up the steps to the next landing, like a cat burglar, advancing on his prey.

He put on his shoes again carefully, without making any noise, and peered into the room. Fleck hadn't heard him! The small man with round spectacles seemed so absorbed in what he was doing that Josh felt able to watch him without fear of being observed. Fleck sat by the window, with his back to the doorway, playing with the ring on his finger. Opposite him sat a large, bearded man strapped in a chair with a makeshift helmet attached to a circlet round his neck. Sir William Feathers had a handkerchief stuffed in his mouth, and his face had gone from red to purple in a struggle to communicate through the handkerchief.

Fleck's cold voice sliced the air. "What are you trying to tell me?" he asked the bearded figure. "I hope for your sake that this is something new or I might be disappointed."

Josh watched as Fleck leaned forward and removed the handkerchief from Sir William's mouth. He saw him give the ring a little twist in an anticlockwise direction and lean back in his seat to observe the results. "It's wonderful, isn't it?" Fleck said, "This sudden release from pain. Think how all this could be yours for ever, if you would only reveal to me what I need to know."

"Then you'd kill me!" gasped Sir William Feathers, with explosive force. "No thanks!"

Fleck toyed with his ring. "You're probably right," he said. "Are you sure you have nothing more to say? Or shall we 'proceed with our enquiries' as the police put it?"

"Go to hell!" said Feathers.

Fleck smiled. "I don't think I'll do that just yet!" he said. "Maybe you wanted to tell me there's a boy at the door." He turned slightly in his chair. "Come where I can see you!" he called out.

Josh stepped forward into the middle of the room, fighting to control his shaking legs.

"Have you met my patient?" said Fleck, not bothering to look round. "His name's Sir William Feathers. Oh, but you knew that, didn't you? He's quite a tough old bird. Would you like me to put him through his paces?"

Sir William stared at him, eyes blazing with a defiant loathing.

"If you carry on sitting in that position any longer," said Josh, still shaking but doing his best to keep an even tone, "you'll probably be shot."

Fleck smiled. Still, he couldn't resist the temptation to stand up and look. "Nice try," he said, returning to his seat. "Now why don't you take a seat beside my friend?"

Josh didn't move.

Fleck studied him with interest. "Ah, you're wondering about the alternative?" he asked. "I suppose I could shoot you with this." He pointed to the pistol on his lap. "Or I could threaten to shoot you. I think that's my preferred option. You see, I need your stones."

"I've only got one," said Josh.

Fleck looked interested. "You may be telling the truth," he said. "That's something we will have to find out."

"I called the police," said Josh.

Fleck licked his lips like a lizard swallowing a fly. "Did you? I expect you did. Then, we'll have to speed things up a little."

Josh felt a sudden fizz of anger that swept away all fear. "They're here now," he said in a firm clear voice. A tremor of excitement ran through his body and he knew it was true.

Fleck gave him a curious sideways glance. "You didn't even look!" he said, shaking his head in mock pity.

"I didn't need to look. I'm the Guardian. I know stuff."

Fleck looked irritated for a moment and walked over to the window. What he saw didn't thrill him. Josh followed his gaze and all his muscles relaxed. The police had arrived. Several of them. Men with loaded rifles emerged from their cars and crouched low as they ran towards the building. They'd even brought a crane. He saw them raising it towards the first-floor window. Well done, Megs! Only she could have stung them into action like this!

Fleck took a few steps backwards and placed himself between Josh and the window frame.

"A marksman," explained Josh, edging away to leave a clear sight of his target. "He's mounting on a platform so that he can get a good view of you. It's not very far away for a good marksman. Even I could shoot you from that distance."

"You'd like that, wouldn't you?" said Fleck, eyes flickering between Josh, the man in the chair and the view from the window, "but then that would trigger off the bomb."

"No, you'd trigger off the bomb," said Josh, gaining in confidence by the minute. "Only you could do that. And nobody could stop you. Trigger off the bomb and you can kill us all."

"Ah, but that would include myself," said Fleck, catching hold of his arm and blinking at him behind his round spectacles. "Maybe you hadn't thought of that?"

"I have another solution," said Josh, shuddering at his touch. "And it would give you the chance to walk out of here alive."

"Let's hear it," said Fleck, blinking again like a lizard. "I like the staying alive bit."

"Wear the circlet yourself. Nobody's going to touch you if you walk out of the house wearing a bomb round your neck."

"And how will they know?" asked Fleck

"I'll tell them," said Josh, taking his phone from his pocket.

Josh watched him weighing up his options. "I like it," he said. In a few quick moves he removed the circlet from his victim's head and placed it round his own.

Josh took out his penknife and cut the rope securing Sir William Feathers to his chair. The explorer rose shakily to his feet and extended a gentlemanly hand to Ronald Fleck. "All's fair in love and war," he said. "Let's shake on it!"

He grabbed Fleck's limp right hand and shook it vigorously, giving the ring a sudden twist which made him gasp and sob with pain. Fleck gave him a vicious look and shot out of the room. Josh stood at the window, beside the huge figure of the bearded explorer, watching Fleck emerge from the house and walk towards a group of guards. Fleck kept up an even pace, ignoring the rifles pointing at him from left and right as if they were toys. When Fleck reached within a few feet of the guards, they saw him stop and speak to the commanding officer. After that, the guards backed off a few paces and shouldered their arms. They pointed Fleck towards the highway leading out of town, where a straggling line of houses ended in open countryside. Instead, Fleck crossed the highway and joined the crowded walking street that led towards the town centre.

"There are no flies on Fleck," commented Sir William grimly. "He wants to mingle with the throng where their snipers daren't pick him out. Let's open a window or two and get some fresh air into our lungs! Ah, that feels better!"

Sir William Feathers took a deep breath, clapped Josh on the back and beamed at his freshly discovered freedom. "I'll tell you one thing, young man," he said with emphasis, sitting down heavily in the wooden chair where he had just been held captive. "I've had some hair-breadth escapes in my life. I've wrestled with a crocodile in the swamps of Amaryllis, I've nearly drowned more than once in the broad, Cassandra river, I've fallen down a cliff face and been left for dead, I've even been chased round a yacht by a madman wielding a harpoon. That was a nasty experience, I can tell you, but nothing beats one hour in an armchair at the mercy of Ronald Fleck. That man has the smell of death on him. Such an insignificant little man too, with those round spectacles and timid little eyes. But behind those eyes – you can sense it – lies the mind of a cobra. Uggh!"

Josh left the window and sat beside the famous explorer. As he did so, he thought he thought he heard a muffled cough coming from the wardrobe on his right. He looked up for a moment, then dismissed it from his mind. "You managed to handle him, Sir William," he said with admiration, looking up at the red, weathered face of the famous explorer.

"Never mind the 'sir' bit. Call me William. In so far as I didn't tell him what he wanted to know, I suppose you are right. Luckily for me, he didn't know that I knew it. Otherwise, the pain might have been worse. I suppose you could say that I led him up the jungle path; I told him that I'd seen young Lucy Fortune in the midst of her tribe, seated on a log surrounded by her family. Fleck got interested at that point. He even turned down the pain for a moment. Then I put in a bit about the stone she wore round her neck."

Feathers paused and clapped a hand to his forehead. "I say, young Josh," he said, "we can't go on talking like this! Don't you think your companions will want to know where you are?"

"Oh, they won't mind," said Josh, absorbed by what Feathers had told him. "There's loads I want to ask you!"

"We've got a bit of time, I suppose. Fire away, young man."

"Where do you think Fleck's heading?"

"He's heading for that jungle in Humphrey's Island. No doubt about that. He's off to find the Fortuna tribe."

"I thought he was working for the Prince. Shouldn't he go to Windfree?"

"He's fallen out of favour with the Prince. He more or less admitted it. I could have guessed the Prince wouldn't put up with his antics for long."

"You sound as if you know him! The Prince, I mean."

Feathers laughed and lit his pipe. He watched the blue smoke drift around the room. "I did know him briefly," he said. "His parents were pirate bankers. Their son attended a posh private school of mainly colonist kids here on this island. I made the mistake of sending my own son there for a year. He got quite friendly with Rupert. We had him home a few times."

"What was he like?"

"A bit serious for a teenager. He got teased a lot – not by my son, I hasten to add. He was into religion and spent a long time studying the *Piratica*. That's why the colonist kids made fun of him – until he knifed one of them, though nobody could ever prove it. He never looked like the kind of kid to knife someone. Well, he's killed plenty of people since his schooldays."

Feathers stopped and held up a hand to one ear. "What's that noise? It sounds like knocking but it doesn't seem to be coming from the door." He stood up and winced. "Ouch! You must excuse me, but my legs are a bit stiff after all that time strapped to a chair."

Josh pointed to a large antique wardrobe. "That's where the sound came from. Listen!"

Feathers limped over and pulled open the two doors. He staggered backward in alarm. "I say, young Josh, I don't know what you must think of me. Bless my soul! There's a beautiful, young lady in this wardrobe. You must think I've been hiding her there all the time, but I swear I had no idea. Come out, young lady, and introduce yourself."

"No need," said Josh, in a sick voice. "I know her. She tried to kill me twice."

The explorer looked first at Miss Cattermole and then at Josh, struggling to control his disbelief. "You?" he said to the Cat Lady. "I mean, is this really true? That you actually tried to kill my young friend?"

The Cat Lady gazed fondly at him. "I only wanted his stone," she said, with a modest shrug. She made herself comfortable in the empty armchair, crossing her long legs and patting her soft, blonde hair into place. She gave Feathers a reassuring smile and folded her delicate, pink hands on her lap.

"She's working with Fleck," warned Josh.

Her eyes settled on Josh's face and flickered away again. "Fleck's finished," she told Feathers. "I have a new master now, and I absolutely adore him. Look! He's given me this."

She inclined her head so that Feathers could see the circlet covered in black velvet that adorned her neck. The four balls round the rim tinkled like bells.

"You're wearing a circlet!" Josh exclaimed.

The Cat Lady nodded with pride. "It's better than the old one," she said. "Do you like it? My master controls the circlets now." Her eyes widened with devotion. "He hardly ever uses them. He's strict, but fair. That's my master all over." She shook her head in admiration at her master's wisdom.

Feathers stood there, legs rooted like tree trunks, stroking his beard and watching the Cat Lady with growing concern. "What were you doing in that wardrobe?" he asked angrily. The Cat Lady looked frightened and bewildered. "Just listening," she said. "I didn't mean any harm."

"But you could have saved me from Fleck."

The Cat Lady gave a frown of concentration. Josh almost felt sorry for her. He could tell she was trying to understand what it felt like to be human. "My master wanted me to stay hidden and listen," she explained. "He's very interested in finding his stone."

Feathers grunted. "Anyway, he didn't learn much, did he?"

The Cat Lady put her head to one side, considering the question. "He learned a little, I suppose, but not enough to find it. My master's very patient, you see. As a matter of fact, he's hoping Josh will be able to find it for him." She turned to Josh, eyes sparkling with tinselly charm. "He'd love to meet you," she said "– in Windfree – I believe that's the next stop on your journey?"

"Does he think the boy's crazy?" Feathers exclaimed. "Why on earth would Josh want to walk into such an obvious trap?"

Josh grinned. "You don't do traps, do you, Miss Cattermole?" he said.

She looked puzzled. "How could he harm you?" she asked, "when you haven't found the other stone? It's not just your stone he needs; it's the whole necklace."

"And what if Fleck finds it first?"

The Cat Lady got up and walked to the window, beckoning to Josh to follow. "That's not going to happen," she said, hugging herself with anticipation as she stared at the sky.

Feathers came and stood behind them at the window, breathing heavily. "What are you looking for?" he asked.

The Cat Lady turned to him. "His private plane," she explained. "The Prince arranged it specially. We won't see much," she sighed, twisting her hands together, "because in a moment the pilot's going to douse him in paraffin and toss his lighted body out of the window – but it's the best we could think of at a moment's notice." She brightened up. "Still, I do like spectacles, don't you? I've been so looking forward to this!" She looked at her watch. "We're a bit early. Another five minutes at least."

Feathers had made up his mind. He went to the far corner of the room and heaved a huge rucksack onto his back. "I don't think we're needed for this," he said.

The Cat Lady clutched his hand. "You're not going, surely? I did so want you to stay and watch the flames. My master didn't want the body to fall over land. He thought it might leave a bad impression, if it landed on someone and he happened to be a pirate."

"Very thoughtful of him!" said Feathers, pulling his hand away. "Unfortunately, I'm not a pirate so I don't feature in his little acts of mercy. I'm off!"

"And taking my friend, Josh, with you?" She turned to Josh. "You will come and visit us in Windfree, won't you? My master insists on meeting you! And I promise no harm will come to you. I give you my word!"

Josh was already halfway out of the door. He smiled. "Could I bring a friend?" he asked.

"Why yes, of course! Is it someone I know? What's his name?"

"Gregory."

"Same age as you or a bit older?"

"A little bit older," said Josh, smiling to himself as he followed Feathers down the stairs.

Together, they walked across the darkening square towards the town centre, Josh slowing his pace to stay abreast of the old man. "Will you join us on the ship?" he asked.

"To help you find Lucy, you mean?" Feathers bent down so that his head was on a level with Josh's. He had a twinkle in his eye. "I think I'll have to," he said. "I don't know how much that strange lady heard in that wardrobe, but it's lucky that she didn't learn enough to find her."

"Isn't she wearing the stone?"

"She's got the stone, all right. Well, she's not wearing it anymore because I advised her against it. But she's not in the jungle anymore. She is working as a cashier in the Hall of Pings. A very sensible young lady. About your age, I'd say."

"I'd hate to work in a Hall of Pings."

"It's a hard world, young Josh. It's part of the Maxtrader chain. Magnus Maxtrader does a lot of business in these parts. The Hall of Pings looked like the best thing going.

"What's she like...Lucy?"

"Tall, fair-haired, long legs. She reminded me of a young giraffe; very willing and sociable."

"Do you think Fleck knows where she is, or the Prince's followers?"

"Nobody knows except me."

They had reached the quayside by now and found Old Surly sitting alone on a bench, his red face glistening with the excitement of the night. Josh had never seen him so animated. He shook Feathers' hands several times, insisting on calling him 'Sir William', and said how he'd learned as a child of his famous adventures. He explained how they'd waited for Josh till long after midnight, with the young lady in tears, fearing for his safety, until they heard the news of his amazing escape. His eyes glittered as he described the shock of seeing a human fireball plunging out of the sky and splashing into the ocean beyond the harbour. Then he coughed and spluttered with laughter and explained that, when they heard that the fireball was Ronald Fleck, they recovered from the shock and decided to throw a party. He pointed towards the ship where the sounds of music and laughter rang out across the waves. "That lot have been partying for the last hour," he told them. He turned to Josh. "I ferried your friends back to the ship the moment we knew you were safe. The young lady wouldn't budge before that." He pointed to the railings where the motor launch was moored. "I think it's time for us to join them."

"What about the captain and Jenkins?" asked Josh.

"Nothing we can do. I can't alter the schedule. We'll just have to leave without them."

As soon as they arrived on board, Josh went off in search of Megs. He found her, sitting under her awning beside the sleeping tiger. But when he tried to tell her about his adventures, she made it quite clear she was not interested in hearing about them.

CHAPTER TWELVE

Josh woke late the next morning, grabbed a quick breakfast and climbed up on deck. He gazed through the unexpected heat haze at the arid rocky landmass shimmering in the midday heat. Despite all the partying, they'd come all this way in one night! They'd arrived in sight of Windfree, the home of the Rebel Prince.

He glanced over at the table where Sandy sat chatting with Megs. Megs was laughing. They seemed to be getting along fine. He felt suddenly alone.

He knew he'd upset Megs. But she wouldn't speak to him. That's what made it so difficult. He knew he should have phoned her. His grip on the railings tightened. He thought of her sitting there, waiting, not knowing if he was dead or alive. He felt hollow in his stomach as he walked towards the table.

"Hi, Megs. Hi Sandy," he said.

Sandy looked up. "Oh. Hi, Josh."

He stood in front of their table and said, in a subdued voice, "I'm sorry, Megs."

Megs flashed a look at him from her under her dark eyelids. "Sorry for what, Josh?" she asked.

"Well, you know; about last night."

Megs stared at him. "I don't know what you are sorry for, Josh. I want you to tell me."

"For forgetting to phone you, I mean."

"Oh, you forgot, did you? So that makes it all right, then?"

"Look, he said he was sorry," Sandy put in.

"You keep out of this," Megs snapped. "This is between me and Josh."

"I should have phoned you," said Josh.

"You didn't have to phone me. You could have phoned Surly. You have his number. You could have phoned Sandy, for all I care."

"I thought it was a bit late."

"And I'd gone to bed? That's what you'd have done, I suppose? Gone to bed and left me with Fleck?"

"No, of course not!"

"So…?"

"I'm sorry, Megs."

"You don't look sorry. What about the police? They saved your life, didn't they?"

"Yes, of course!"

"Do you think they came because of you – because of your one little phone call?"

"I don't know. Do you mean…?"

"Yes! Sandy and I rushed down to the station. I had to shout and scream to get their attention."

"I don't think they liked all that shouting," said Sandy quietly, keeping his head down.

"I told you to keep out of this, Sandy!"

Josh stood there feeling small and awkward. "Yes, well you saved my life, Megs," he said. "And I should have phoned to say I was safe. I didn't think. And now I am really sorry. And will you give me a break, Megs, please?"

"I don't know, Josh. I'll have to think about it."

She tried to hide the glimmer of a smile. He began to relax.

Sandy dared to look up. "Have you finished?" he asked. "I want to show you something." He pulled a piece of paper out of his pocket which he unfolded with pride. "There! I've written it out for you," he said, "Five reasons why you shouldn't see the Prince."

"You're not you really planning to see him, are you?" asked Megs.

Josh could see from the way she looked at Sandy that they'd been talking about it. He hesitated. "I don't know," he explained. "There isn't time."

Megs gave a teasing laugh. "Yes, well, of course. You're so busy! Princes have to stand in line like the rest of us."

Josh squirmed. "No, of course I didn't mean that. It's just ...." His voice tailed away. "Go on then, Sandy, let's hear it."

"Number One," read Sandy, checking to see if he was free to speak yet. "The Prince wants to see you." He waited to see Josh's reaction.

Josh laughed. "Is that it? He wants to see me. What's that supposed to prove?"

"He has something to gain from seeing you. If he thought that you'd got anything to gain from seeing him, he wouldn't invite you."

Josh rolled that one round in his mind. He couldn't work out if it made sense.

Sandy went back to his paper. "Number Two. You think you're safe because he hasn't got the other stones yet, but what if he knows where to find them?"

Josh opened his mouth to say something, but thought better of it. Sandy looked down at his paper again. "Number three. He's cunning. He could turn this into a propaganda coup. What if he has witnesses and uses the meeting to prove that you support his cause?"

"I thought of that one," said Megs.

"Good thinking," said Josh, "but how would it help him?"

"Well, I'm not a pirate," explained Sandy, "but, I mean, you're the Guardian! Besides, your family are sort of square as far as pirates go. If it can be proved that you support the Prince, it will widen his appeal – you know, make him respectable among the traditional kind of pirates; the ones that have jobs and stuff."

"But the Prince is respectable too. He's the son of a banker. That's what Feathers told me."

"Is he? Yea, but he comes across as a rebel." Sandy went back to his list. "Number Four. He could just grab you, fit you up with a circlet and force you to help him find the other stones."

"But Gregory will be with me!"

"Yes, but they're armed. They could shoot him."

"He's a talking tiger! The Prince's reputation would be ruined."

"He controls his reputation. Don't you see? On his home turf, he could explain away Gregory's death any way he chooses." Sandy laid his paper on the table. "Well, that's about it," he said with a grin.

"What about number five?"

"Oh yes, number five. He could kidnap you and leave us lot to risk our lives trying to rescue you."

"I assure you that's not going to happen!" boomed Feathers, emerging from the hatchway. He slowly approached the table, leaning heavily on a stick and supported on the other side by Frederic Forbes.

"Where are the others?" Josh whispered to Megs.

"There are no others except for Bosworthy," she whispered back. "Tuffers never meant to return. He's cleared out his room."

"Great!"

Feathers sat down heavily at the table. "Excuse the stick," he grunted. "Fleck put me through my paces yesterday." His eyes fell on the paper in Sandy's hand. "Mind if I have a look?"

Sandy blushed and handed it over. "It's just a few ideas we put together," he said.

"I must say that you've given it some thought," said Forbes, leaning over Feathers' shoulder. "'The Prince wants to see you!' That's very good." He turned to Feathers. "If it's good for the Prince, it can't be good for Josh. I do see their point." He came and sat beside Feathers at the table. "Very true!" he murmured, and "Quite right!" as his eyes ran down the page.

Feathers groped in his jacket for a pair of spectacles and read through the paper a second time. Finally, he cleared his throat and looked at Sandy. "Well done, my boy!" he said, returning the paper. "I like your five points; all of them."

"Megs thought of them, too."

"Well done, Megs. Only, I'm afraid there's a point six. If the Prince wants to see Josh, we can't stop him. Look over there! You see that? That's Crackbones Harbour."

Josh turned in his seat. The ship was making its stately progress toward the walled harbour entrance. He could see a large crowd lining the quays.

"That's our reception committee," said Feathers. "I expect the Prince's men are among them."

"So, you mean that list was a waste of time?" asked Megs.

"Well, the Prince controls the seas in these parts. He could blow us out of the water if it suited his purpose. And Humphrey's Island is a stone's throw from Windfree. He controls that too. So we can't really stop him from seeing Josh. We just have to exercise common sense."

"I don't get that bit," said Josh.

Feathers searched the air for an explanation, "Common sense," he said "Hm. Well, if you're being chased by a madman waving an axe, do what he asks. That's common sense."

"What if he wants to kill Josh?" asked Sandy. "Josh can do nothing about it."

Feathers laughed. "I see you people are one step ahead of me," he said. "Well, I think Josh is safe for the moment. He wants Josh in order to get those other stones."

"How will I find him?" asked Josh.

"Oh, I don't think there's a question of finding him. He will send someone to pick us up."

Josh looked across at the harbour and the blue hills beyond, shimmering in the heat. He wondered about his meeting with the Prince. If the Prince asked him about the stone of love, what could he say? He couldn't tell him where to find it. In that case, the Prince would end the meeting at once. He'd seize the stone Josh possessed and go off in search of the other one. But if he refused to answer, would that make the Prince angry? Would he threaten him? In front of Gregory? Josh looked across at the aged tiger, snoozing in the heat. He was glad to have Gregory as a companion.

Behind him, he heard an enthusiastic chuckle from Frederic Forbes. "Windfree!" exclaimed Forbes, rocking forward on his seat. "Windfree! What an unusual name! What can you tell us about this island, Sir William?"

Feathers coughed and removed his glasses. "I suppose I should begin," he said "by explaining lack of wind was not something that greatly appealed to Captain Crackbones. His crew were stuck here in the searing heat of a Windfree summer – and all because they never had enough wind to fill their sails."

He looked up and raised a hand to welcome John Bosworthy, who quietly took his place at the table.

"Most interesting!" exclaimed Frederic Forbes. "I must confess I never heard that explanation. I must make a note of it."

Josh nodded and stood up. "When are we leaving?" he asked. "If I've got to see the Prince, let's get it over with now."

Feathers held up a hand. "Steady on, young Josh." He pointed towards the harbour. "If you wanted to leave now, you'd have to swim. I can't say I'd be very eager to join you. Better wait for the ship to dock, eh? And then…well, then, I'm sure the Prince will send someone to pick us up. I think it's time for us to prepare for the visit." He rose to his feet. "A change of clothes might be advisable," he added, looking at Sandy. "It's extremely hot and we may need to do some walking."

Forbes touched him on the shoulder. "If you'll excuse me, I fear I won't be much use to you in this heat. I think I will retire to my cabin and write up my journal."

Feathers nodded. "Everyone except my friend, Forbes, then," he said, as they all got up from the table. "I'd just like to have a word in private with young Josh."

As the others departed, Feathers sat down again. He winked at Josh. "We can't be too careful," he said. "I have something to show you that is for your eyes only."

"Tufton's gone."

"Ah, yes. But what about the crew? Do we know them? A chance word could easily be overheard by one of the sailors." He unfolded a hand-drawn map of Windfree. "It's not the meeting with the Prince that worries me," he confided. "It's what comes afterwards. I don't think we can afford to come back to the ship after the meeting."

"Why not?"

"Why not?" Feathers took out his pipe and tobacco pouch. Soon the sweet, smoky aroma wafted across the deck. "Because," he continued, "it would take us too long." He took another puff and pointed to the right-hand edge of his map. "Here's the Prince's encampment; only a stone's throw from Humphrey's Island. If the Prince doesn't get what he wants – and, knowing you, young Josh, I'm sure he won't – he'll ferry his troops over there so that they're ready and waiting for us to arrive. They'll follow your search for the stone and seize you as soon as you've found it. That's why we have to get there quickly."

Feathers pointed at a spot near the eastern tip of the island. "You see that bay?" he asked. "It's only a mile or so from the encampment. That's Wolf's Cove, where Old Surly will be waiting for us in an old motor launch." He looked at his watch.

"He's probably there already," he said. "The others can return to the ship. Let's hope the Prince thinks that we've done the same."

"But how do we get to that cove without being spotted?

"That's the difficult bit," admitted Feathers. "He rose shakily to his feet. "I expect our escort will be here soon," he said. "Better keep this a secret between ourselves, eh?"

Chapter Thirteen

T he Prince's envoy dropped them at the harbour, telling them to proceed out of the town to the Hall of Pings. From there, the Prince's limousine would take them to his encampment in the east.

Josh felt Megs' arm hugging his elbow. With the sun beating down on his head and his shirt sticking to his chest, he could have done without that extra, nagging pressure, but he knew what it meant. *While I'm l here, nobody's going to mess with you!* He pressed her arm to his side, grateful for her support.

"Are you going to take the stone with you?" she asked.

With his free arm he wiped the sweat from his brow. "I dunno, Megs," he said.

Josh didn't think it mattered. The Prince could do what he wanted on his own patch but he didn't just want his stone – he could seize that any time. So why did the Prince want to see him? It couldn't be for anything good.

"Do you think Feather's plan will work?" she asked.

"Sh! The others aren't supposed to know."

"Not even Sandy?"

"Feathers says not even Sandy – it's best if nobody knows. Then, if they get questioned, they don't have to pretend. Sandy's not very good at pretending," he added.

"But you told me."

 "Yes, but you're different."

Megs gave his hand another squeeze.

They'd left the crowded main road and followed a parallel, dusty path bordered on either side by a rocky wasteland. In the distance, above the harbour, a dark green line of trees stretched as far as the eye could see. "What are those?" he asked Bosworthy.

Bosworthy wiped his glasses and scanned the horizon. In his checked shirt and shorts, he looked like an overgrown schoolboy who'd lost his way in the desert. "Oh, that's gunge," he said. "All that belongs to Magnus Maxtrader. In fact, the only products that grow on this arid scrubland are the forget-me flower and gunge. Between them, the Prince and Maxtrader hold the economy in the palms of their hands."

"What's gunge?" asked Josh.

Feathers had caught up with them now. He had one hand on his walking stick and used the other to wipe the sweat dripping down his red face onto his grey beard. He glanced at Josh to see if he was joking. "Are you honestly telling me you've never heard of gunge?" he asked.

"I'm not very good on trees," Josh admitted.

"Well, it's more like a bush, really. It produces a white fluffy substance, a bit like cotton, but of a rubbery texture. The great thing about gunge – well, there's two great things actually – it's absolutely tasteless and it can be moulded like clay. You look doubtful, Josh. I don't blame you!"

"Why would people want to eat clay?" asked Josh.

"Good question! The point is that you can turn it into any shape you want: chicken, steak, roast beef, puddings, bread, sweets…you name it! Of course, you have to add flavour. That's done in the taste laboratories where they add chemicals to make the stuff taste like chicken, strawberries or the like. Of course, over the years the process gets easier."

"Why?"

"Because people have forgotten what real chicken and strawberries taste like."

"What about colour?"

"Oh, that's the easy bit! That's all done in the dyeing factories."

"Have you ever tasted gunge?" asked Josh.

"Of course I have! So have you, though you may not be aware of it. Have you ever bought any food from Maxtraders recently?"

"All the supermarkets on Colony Island are Maxtraders."

"Well, there you are. All gunge!"

Bosworthy pointed ahead towards a small township of rectangular factories clustered round one enormous hall with a glass dome, visible for miles, shimmering in the heat. "Those are the gunge factories," he said, "and that dome is the 'Rebel Prince', a brand-new Hall of Pings named after 'guess who?'.

"When does it open?" asked Josh.

"In about an hour. That gives us plenty of time."

Behind him, Josh heard a low, tigerish whine like the sound of a saw cutting through metal.

"He's hungry," said Megs, releasing Josh's arm. "Shall we stop for something to eat?"

They sat in friendly silence among a clump of sun-warmed rocks at the side of the path. Gregory sniffed the air with interest. He'd nobly consented to wear a collar attached to a long length of rope; a great indignity for a talking tiger, but people weren't used to tigers in Windfree.

He was enough of an old pro to use it to his advantage. "If my dear mother were alive to witness this event," he said, "she would say it served me right. Let it be a judgement on me for my misspent youth that an aged tiger should be dragged in chains through a hostile land."

"What's he saying?" asked Bosworthy.

"He's offended by that rope," Josh whispered, "and hungry, too. You've got a steak in that bag for him, haven't you, Megs?"

"I suppose a steak might be good for me in my condition," said the tiger with a brave show of reluctance.

The only sound for quite a while was the crackle of raw meat being wrenched apart by a satisfied tiger. Megs listened with an air of rapt contentment. She looked happy sitting by the tiger's side. Josh thought she enjoyed the experience almost as much as the tiger.

Suddenly, above the steady roar of traffic, they could hear loud cheering and the honking of horns. "Those are the Shopalots," said Bosworthy, "the natives of Windfree. Those bubble cars they're driving are shop mobiles and they're all heading for the Hall of Pings." The Shopalots passed in droves, one person to each mini vehicle, weaving in and out of each other in their effort to gain an advantage in their race to the hall.

"Some of them are very fat!" cried Megs.

"Succulent," suggested Gregory, who had finished his meat and sniffed the air in mock anticipation. Megs reached over and threatened to hit him.

"They are a naturally big-boned race," said Bosworthy, "but in the past they used to keep themselves in trim by back-breaking labour in the fields. Those times are over now. They're all working in the gunge factories and existing on a diet of gunge."

"Why have they got chains round their necks?" asked Josh.

"Oh! Those are for the 'net worth' tabs," said Feathers. "Do you see them? Those little metal squares with numbers on them; they're calculators. They don't use money in Windfree. When they collect their goods from the Hall of Pings, the cashier just waves the bill in front of the tab and the total is deducted from their net worth; the amount they've earned from working in the gunge factories. It's a very simple system," he added, "like slavery."

They'd reached the township now and had to make their way past the factories. Each building had the name 'Magnus Maxtrader' picked out in large red letters along the side, with the description of the product underneath – 'Cereals and Desserts,' 'Beef and Poultry', "Fruit and Vegetables'…"

The shouts and screams and honking of horns became deafening as they approached the Hall of Pings. At that moment, the doors of the great hall slid open and the ping of a thousand bar codes rang out above the cries and honking of horns as the Shopalots drove into the building.

"Ah! Here's what we came for," cried John Bosworthy. He pointed up the road at a black stretched limo with tinted windows approaching the hall. The Shopalots in their shop mobiles scattered to the sides of the road, leaving a respectful space for the Prince's stretched limo. The spectators in their shop mobiles shouted to Bosworthy to get out of the way, but he just stood there, staring with vague curiosity at the oncoming limo until, with a soft sigh like the sound of a fat man settling into an armchair, it subsided at his feet.

A chauffeur in a blue uniform and peaked hat stepped out of the vehicle. "Are you the party to see the Prince?" he asked. Feathers nodded. "And is this the boy? He'd better go in the front seat, then." He opened the door for Josh to squeeze in beside Feathers. Then he turned to Sandy and Megs and waved them into the seat behind. "How many more?" he asked Sandy.

"Just two."

"Ah, yes, two. And one of them's Gregory. A tiger," he added. He didn't sound especially fond of tigers. He closed the door and stood at attention beside his limousine.

"We're locked in," said Sandy.

Josh sensed a trap. It wouldn't be easy to get off this island. The Prince seemed to know all their moves in advance. How else would his driver know that Gregory was a tiger? He sank back into the comfort of his leather seat and tried to relax.

At that moment, he heard a sudden thud as the chauffeur fell backwards against the side of his door. "I don't think he's used to tigers," he whispered to Feathers.

The chauffeur struggled to regain his poise and opened a third door at the back of the limousine, where the seat had been taken out and a thick tartan rug laid over the floor. Gregory clambered aboard, stretched out his ageing limbs on the rug and snuffled and twitched for a while as he settled into a deep sleep. Once again Josh heard a click and they were locked in.

"Where's Bosworthy?" asked Megs.

Josh pointed towards a parking lot at the side of the Hall of Pings. He'd been watching John Bosworthy with a camera over his shoulder, darting around two lorries, marked 'Magnus Maxtrader – Food Supplies'. After taking a rapid series of snapshots of each lorry with its Maxtrader logo, he managed to open the back of one of the lorries and take photos of the goods inside. He emerged and spotted the limousine and came hurrying back towards them.

"Take a look at these!" he whispered, scrambling into a seat beside Megs. He reached over to show his photographs to Feathers. "That's all the evidence I need. Those lorries belong to Magnus Maxtrader and they're stuffed full of 'medical supplies'; in other words '*Oblivia Preciosa.*'"

"I don't understand," said Josh, turning to Bosworthy.

"What don't you understand, Josh?"

"I mean how he can get away with dealing in that stuff? Don't you get arrested for that sort of thing?"

"The plant has its medical uses but it's also a lethal poison," explained John Bosworthy. "The trade has be strictly regulated. I don't think Maxtrader's neighbours would like to know that the Prince is selling this stuff in exchange for weapons which may be used against them."

"Does Magnus Maxtrader know about this?"

Bosworthy laughed. "Well, maybe his business empire has grown so big that he doesn't know what his subordinates are doing," he said. "I'm here to help him find out!"

"Will he be in trouble?"

"In the long run, yes – unless he's got an extremely good lawyer, which he probably has."

The driver climbed into the limo, secured all the doors and drove in silence away from the Hall of Pings. For the next two hours, the limo sped noiselessly past an unchanging view of reddish sand and rocks and stunted trees. This was the semi-desert of central Windfree. Josh gazed out of the open window until the flat monotony of the landscape got the better of him and he nearly fell asleep.

"Watch out!" cried Feathers. "Close all the windows!"

Too late. A rich, rotting smell invaded Josh's nostrils. Megs screamed and held her hands to her face. Out of the window, Josh saw a line of creatures the size of buffaloes lumbering towards the limo with ugly tusks like giant corkscrews.

"Those are yucks!" explained Feathers. "They're quite harmless. If we just drive on, they'll get the message and move aside for us."

"They smell foul!" Megs protested.

"Look out! There's thousands of them!" cried Josh. He saw a cloud of dust in the distance, half concealing a solid, brown mass thundering along after their leaders.

"Better drive faster!" Feathers advised the chauffeur. "Yucks don't change direction in a hurry," he explained to his fellow passengers. "They've got remarkably small brains. By the time they get here, we'll be well past." He turned round in his seat. "Funny thing," he said. "Yucks seem to be on the increase. I suppose that's because they have no natural predators. A bit like humans."

"We've got each other," John Bosworthy reminded him.

The leading line of yucks had nearly reached the limo. The chauffeur honked his horn which made them stop and change direction, giving a plaintive yuck moo like a herd of moody bullocks. Josh watched them through the back window dwindling into a thin brown smudge on the dusty landscape.

"How much longer?" he asked.

"Not long!" said Feathers. "We will soon be entering the Prince's domain. There's a bridge up ahead over the River Sandmoss. It's the only river in Windfree and its waters irrigate the flower plantations which will come into view shortly. You'll be seeing red for a few miles. After that, the road slopes upwards towards the Kraak mountains where the rebel army hangs out."

Josh sat up and looked around him, absorbing every detail. They had crossed the bridge now and were passing through the flower plantations, where men on horseback rode up and down the hedgerows, shouting orders at the Shopalots, gathering the flowers in baskets and loading them onto trailers.

"The factory is up ahead!" observed Feathers. "And those men in uniform loitering by the lorries parked in the factory yard – they're all rebel soldiers. The lorries, on the other hand – do you see them? – belong to Magnus Maxtrader. That's what I call true co-operation! I hope you're still taking photographs, Bosworthy?"

"Of course, I am! This will create quite a stir, I can tell you."

Very soon they left the plantations behind them and came to the foothills of the Kraak mountains. "Those are to house the latest recruits," explained Feathers, indicating rows and rows of brown army ridge tents pitched on the dusty plain. He pointed to the foothills beyond where a number of identical white bungalows had been built or were in the process of construction. "After a few weeks, they'll be able to move into those houses and new recruits will arrive from Crown Colony, Colony Island – you name it – to occupy the tents." He sighed.

"Yes, the rebel army is growing, thanks to the arms trade and Magnus Maxtrader!"

The road came to a stop in a gravelled parking lot in the foothills.

"This is it," the captain said quietly to Josh. "The Prince has agreed to meet you here. He'll take you to his bungalow up in the hills and, after the meeting, he'll guide you back down again. That's where the rest of us will be waiting. Just take my advice and say as little as possible. Let him do the talking."

As soon as they stepped out of the limo, Josh could hear the shouts and cheers of a public gathering, masked by the trees away to his left. "They're celebrating the anniversary of the rebel army," Feathers explained. "It's mainly shooting and climbing under barbed wire. That sort of thing. They use real bullets and sometimes shoot each other by mistake. It's called friendly fire."

Just at that moment the trees parted and a troop of piratical soldiers, wearing the Prince's insignia of long white robes with the letters 'RR' embroidered on their chests and with rifles slung over their shoulders, took up positions on either side of the parking lot. Everyone went still.

Then the trees parted again and a tall, slender young man in white robes, but without the insignia, entered the parking lot, accompanied by an officer with a large red face and very white hair. The troops puffed out their chests, all eyes on their leader. Josh noticed the fanatical devotion in those eyes. Then one of them inclined his head to reveal the brass rim of a circlet. He took a closer look at the others. They all wore circlets!

With the casual ease of a man in total command, the Prince ignored his troops and strolled over to speak to Josh. "At last! I've been expecting you!" he said in a soft voice.

Josh managed to nod. The Prince was younger than he expected and his brown eyes drew you into his orbit. For a while, nobody spoke. Then the Prince smiled. "Josh Flagsmith," he said, stepping forward and imprisoning Josh's hand in two of his own. Josh felt a shiver run through him. "I have heard nothing but good things about you," said the Prince, "and I am most looking forward to our little chat; just the two of us and the noble tiger who was alive in the time of my great ancestor." He gave Josh a probing stare. "You see, I haven't forgotten Gregory," he said. Josh felt as if he'd been caught cheating. How did the Prince know that Gregory was a tiger? And what would he do to him?

The Prince turned to Sandy and Megs. He seemed especially intrigued by Megs. "Do you mind my having a private word with Josh?" he asked.

Megs gave him a hard stare. "Do you mind if I mind?" she asked.

Josh winced. The Prince just turned away to chat with John Bosworthy; he seemed to know him by name. Then he talked and laughed with Feathers, reminding him of the days he spent at his house during his school days. Josh noticed that the Prince did most of the laughing. Finally, the Prince waved Feathers and Bosworthy goodbye and turned to Josh again. He threw an arm over his shoulder and led him up some steps to the right of the path. "My house," he explained. "It's not very far, if Gregory wouldn't mind following us." Josh was glad to hear the tiger padding along behind them.

The Prince's bungalow was the highest among several similar white bungalows dotted around the mountainside. Josh entered a simple, square room with white walls, furnished with two armchairs on either side of the only window and a sofa facing it. "Cast offs from my foster-parents' house in Crown Colony," the Prince explained, "in the days when we were still on speaking terms." He looked quite boyish when he said that, and Josh felt like his equal. The walls of the room were covered with maps, charts, drawings and old oil paintings relating to piratical history.

Josh's eyes were drawn to an elaborate family tree tracing the Prince's descent from Rupert the Rebel.

"By all means, feel free to look around," said the Prince. "I see you're admiring my ancestor."

Opposite the window stood a painting similar to the one Josh had seen in the museum on Colony Island. The likeness to his host was uncanny.

"What's the castle in the background?" he asked.

The Prince came and stood behind him. "Oh, that! Don't you recognize it?" he asked. "It's my ancestor's castle on Colony Island. I'm hoping to have it restored."

Josh looked round. Was he serious? Did that mean he planned to take over the island?

The Prince laughed, reading his thoughts. "Only if I'm invited to," he said.

Invited to do what? Restore the castle or take over the island?

The Prince pointed to a large map on the left of the picture entitled 'Colonist Invasions in the time of Rupert the Rebel.' A red arrow depicted as a serpent's tongue started from the great continent in the east and forked out into smaller arrows aimed at each of the western isles, coming to a final sharp point in Colony Island.

"That's what the colonists did to us," said the Prince, "and that's what my great ancestor tried to stop." His eyes filled with bitterness.

Josh wandered round the room, studying the maps and charts. He noticed the closed door behind the Prince's armchair. He opened it a fraction. He heard a quick rustle of feet and felt the Prince's arm over his shoulder, slamming it shut. "Not in there!" said the Prince with a laugh. "That's my prayer room!"

Josh muttered a quick "Sorry!" and pretended to take an interest in another wall chart.

Some prayer room! His heart thumped as he struggled to hide how much he'd seen; a huge, cavernous space with tunnels leading underground, where rebel soldiers strode around with rifles slung over their shoulders, while others manned telephones and clicked away at computers.

The Prince turned his attentions to Gregory. He bent over his great neck and made him comfortable on the sofa. "This is a first for me!" he announced, clapping his long hands together, "meeting this magnificent tiger who lived in the times of my great ancestor. I have been so looking forward to this visit!" He straightened up and smiled at Josh with his sad brown eyes, directing him to an armchair.

"Can I offer you some tea? It's all we drink here, I'm afraid. No? None for me either. How about our famous tiger?"

Josh saw that Gregory had fallen asleep. 'So much for my protection!' he thought.

The Prince sat in the armchair opposite, drawing his white robes round him. "Isn't the view magnificent, with the sun just beginning to set in the mountain and those red fields of forget-me flowers – do you see them? – which give off such a beautiful scent in the early evening?"

Josh followed his gaze. With thumping heart, thinking of all those soldiers in the cavern beyond that door, he felt bound to protest. "Aren't those poisonous?" he asked.

The Prince looked sad for a moment. "They can be used as a poison," he said, "but, if treated in a laboratory, they have important medical uses. I leave that side of things to my friend, Magnus Maxtrader." He examined his fingernails.

Josh felt a shiver of unease. "But don't you sell this stuff in exchange for weapons?" he asked.

The Prince sighed. "Ah, the lengths to which I have to go to restore the pride of the pirate race. Weapons! Yes, I'm as sorry as you are, Josh, that we have to resort to such trade."

Josh risked one last question on the subject. "That can't be quite right, can it?" he asked. "I mean, you can't say you are as sorry as I am because you don't know how sorry I would be – if I were in your position, I mean."

"That's one way of looking at it," agreed the Prince.

Josh wondered what the other way was, but the Prince was still smiling at him, so he smiled back. "I suppose you need the money to buy gunge to feed your troops too," he suggested.

The Prince nodded and leaned forward in his chair. "You and I understand one another, Josh," he said. "It's terrible stuff, this gunge. One day I would like to burn the lot of it. In fact, that's what I'm thinking of doing." His eyes sparkled. "Can you imagine? All the gunge that grows on Humphrey's Island and Windfree! I intend to send it up in smoke – so much for the colonist dreams of Magnus Maxtrader!"

Josh began to think that the Prince was mad. Didn't he realize that if you destroyed all the gunge, people would starve? Then he took another look at those wide, sincere, eyes and he saw that the Prince did realize! "What will people eat?" he asked.

The Prince shrugged. "The colonists, you mean?" He looked down at his clean fingernails. "We pirates have little enough to eat, as it is. I suppose they will have to start going back where they came from. As for us – pirates, I mean – we will go back to the way things used to be four hundred years ago before a single colonist set foot in this island."

Gregory creaked and groaned on the sofa and raised his great head. "Why stop there?" he enquired. "Why not eight hundred? Why draw a line in the sands of history and say that we must all go back to one particular time and not another?"

The Prince looked interested. "Why eight hundred?"

Josh realised to his amusement that Gregory had been awake all the time. "Eight hundred years or longer is the time we animals have been known to exist on Amaryllis," the tiger explained, "long before the first pirates landed on our shores."

"No, no, no!" exclaimed the Prince, leaning forward on his chair. You could tell this was the sort of discussion he loved.

"The pirates were always meant to rule the western isles, not that we ever minded sharing them with the talking animals. You just have to read the *Piratica*."

"But what if other humans come along that haven't read the *Piratica*?" asked Gregory. "Or what if they are simple tigers like myself that can't read? Do they have to move because it says so in your book?"

"That's a good point," said the Prince, deciding to ignore it. "Now, you're a clever fellow," he said to Josh. "Great ideas! What an interesting world we could create between us once we restore that necklace!"

Silence descended on the room. Josh felt the Prince's watchful eyes upon him and realised this was why he'd been asked to come. He struggled for an answer.

The tiger got there first. "Sharing is a wonderful quality," he said, lifting his great head once again. "But if you are planning to share a necklace, laudable as the idea might seem, wouldn't you need to share the same neck?"

The Prince stared at him. The friendliness had gone out of his eyes.

"I venture to suggest that young Josh is contented with his single stone," continued Gregory, rising on to his four paws. "That is really all he desires; to head home to Amaryllis and leave these weightier matters to a Prince like yourself."

The Prince nodded and stood up. "I bow to the wisdom of an ancient tiger," he said. "We can't both have the necklace. Now, if you'll forgive me, I normally say my prayers at this time of the evening so I'd be obliged if you'd let yourselves out."

The audience was suddenly at an end.

Chapter Fourteen

When Josh led Gregory back to the parking lot, he saw the limousine waiting in the shadow of the trees. Sandy was smiling about something. He pointed at the limo. "Have you seen our new chauffeur?" he asked. The man's back was turned. He looked thinner and taller than Josh remembered and, as he bent over the machine, his bare legs stuck out from his blue trouser bottoms. Then the man turned round, and Josh found himself staring into the friendly face of John Bosworthy.

"I've never driven anything this large before," said Bosworthy, scratching his head with an air of amused perplexity. "I can give it a try."

Josh looked at Megs. "Where's the real chauffeur?" he asked.

"Feathers hit him with a brick," said Megs.

"Don't exaggerate," said Sandy.

"Well, he hit him with something." She pointed to the man sitting gagged and bound in the back seat of the limo. "They had to silence him, but it wasn't pretty. How did it go with the Prince?"

"No time, no time!" cried Feathers, panting and red in the face as he emerged from the limo. "Climb in, everyone. We have to get out of here fast!"

"But what about the chauffeur?" asked Sandy.

"He goes with you, back to the ship. We can't leave him here." Feathers looked at them in exasperation. "Don't you hear the cheers? That means the ceremony's over, and the soldiers will be heading this way any moment."

Josh rushed to the rear door for Gregory to clamber aboard and hurried into the front beside Feathers. Sandy and Megs jumped into the seat beside the chauffeur, who'd been gagged and bound. The limo lurched onto the main road and headed down the slope towards the trees that bordered the Prince's domain. As soon as they were safely hidden among the trees, Josh gave a breathless account of the meeting, explaining what he'd seen in the Prince's prayer room and how Gregory had come to his rescue at the end.

"If you want to share the same necklace, you need to share the same neck!" mused Feathers. "Well done, Gregory! What a splendid answer!" He turned to Bosworthy. "With any luck, the Prince will imagine we've all gone back to the ship," he said. "Slow up, now! We're coming to a bend. This is where Josh and I get off."

Bosworthy stopped the limo just long enough for Josh and Feathers to get out. Josh felt a sharp pang of sadness as he gave one last wave to Sandy and Megs and watched the limo swerve round the bend and disappear from view. Even if all went well, he knew he wouldn't see them again until the ship docked in Amaryllis. He turned and followed Feathers down a narrow, overgrown path through the woods. The road was soon lost to sight, and even the noise of traffic dwindled to a distant roar. In the dim light, Feathers picked his way with care, stopping at intervals to check the direction. At one point, after looking at his compass, he turned and retraced his steps, hurrying down a different path which led directly south towards the sea. Josh wondered if they would ever make it to the cove. As if to guess his thoughts, Feathers called out, "Two hours before sundown.

No need to hurry. We can't leave the island before it gets dark. We might be spotted."

After the dry heat of the day, this felt like another world. Few rays of sunlight trickled through the leaves. Tall trees surrounded them for miles on all sides, dropping their cooling moisture on the thick brown leaf-mould which squelched underfoot.

"We'll come to some steps soon," said Feathers, grabbing a sapling for balance as he came to a halt. "The first pirates built them nearly 400 years ago. I climbed them once, but that was twenty years ago. They are very steep and slippery, so we'll have to be careful. Sh! Did you hear something?"

Somewhere in the distance ahead of them, Josh thought he heard voices. They sounded thin and shrill, like children playing in the woods. Feathers listened for a bit. "Nothing we need worry about," he decided. "Probably natives; hunter gatherers that live in these woods. Not everyone has opted for the gunge plantations and the Halls of Pings. Let's move on."

"Do you think the Prince will be waiting for us?" asked Josh.

"Let's hope not. If he thinks we've gone back to the ship, he doesn't need to hurry." The ground sloped downwards now, and more light filtered through the trees. Josh thought about the Cat Lady picking her way through that jungle in the north of Humphrey's Island. Would she do that or would she head straight into the town and ask for a girl with fair hair called Lucy Fortune? And what if she found her? She couldn't have found her yet! That was obvious from his meeting with the Prince.

"Not long now!" Feathers called out. In the distance, Josh could make out specks of light where the woods ended and the cliffs began. The thought of sailing overnight excited him. Feathers had said they would get there before dawn.

"Where will we land?" he asked.

Feathers turned round. He fished a soiled rag from his pocket and mopped his brow. "I know a little cove a mile or so up the coast from the harbour," he said. "It's not far from the Hall of

Pings where Lucy works." He paused. "That's if she still works there," he added.

Josh felt a stab of doubt. He struggled to push the thought away from him. Of course, she still worked there! She probably had no choice. And if she didn't, surely his stone would help him to find her? He looked darkly at Feathers, who'd already moved some distance ahead of him. Why did the old man need to sow doubts in his mind?

"What if she doesn't want to surrender her stone?" he asked.

Feathers stopped again and started searching the undergrowth. "Don't worry about that," he said. "She knows it's yours. I told her to expect you one day. Besides, she's not like the Prince. She knows those stones are no use to anyone but yourself. Now where are those steps?" He wandered off the path and kicked away some of the rough grass until his boots tapped on rough brick. "Here we are," he said. "This is the roofed archway. It collapsed a long time ago so we have to skirt round it and join the steps further down. After that, it's easy enough. The steps descend for about fifty feet in one direction and then turn in the other direction and so on until we reach the cove. Careful! I don't know if they were giants in those days, but the steps are very steep. I'll have to take them slowly, I'm afraid, or I won't be able to walk for a week."

"How many steps are there?" asked Josh.

Feathers grunted. "762!" he said. "I counted them."

"Let me go first!" said Josh. He winced at the thought of Feathers struggling down those steps. To his surprise, the old man moved aside for him. The descent didn't look too difficult. The steps were cut into the sides of a wide treeless slope so that you could make out the sea in the distance but, if you slipped, you couldn't fall far. Josh counted out fifty steps and then stopped. He looked back and saw Feathers climbing down backwards, using the steps above to maintain his balance.

"Fifty!" said Feathers, coming to rest on the fiftieth step. "You don't notice it at first but the height of each step plays havoc with your knees. I'm afraid I'm not as nimble as you, young Josh." He took a swig from his water bottle and cautioned Josh to do the same. "It's hotter than you think," he said.

"I'll go a bit slower this time," said Josh, starting down the next set of steps which curved round and descended in the opposite direction. He kept turning to observe the old man's painful progress. Ninety steps, one hundred, one hundred and ten. They'd only just started! Feathers clambered down and sat beside him on the hundred and twentieth step. He mopped his brow and took another swig of water.

"What's that noise?" asked Josh. Soon they both heard it; a sound like the steady drone of locusts overhead, the sound of helicopters heading eastward.

"Too bad!" muttered Feathers. "The Prince hasn't wasted any time. They'll be all over the island by the time we arrive."

"Do you think he knows we haven't gone to the ship?" asked Josh.

Feathers stroked his beard. "I wouldn't imagine so," he said, "but he needs time to deploy his troops over a very wide area. Let's hope we get there before he's ready for us!"

For a while, they continued in silence, stopping at intervals for Feathers to rest. After a time, even Josh felt his legs begin to wobble with the effort of climbing down one foot at a time. On the four hundredth step, Feathers sat down heavily and massaged his joints. He panted and perspired and looked at his watch. "I'm sorry, Josh," he said. "You'll have to go on ahead at your own speed and tell Surly that we're here; otherwise, he won't wait. I'll make it down somehow at my own pace."

Josh hesitated.

"Go on!" the old man insisted. "I've been in worse situations than this. I can manage!"

Josh reached in his pocket for his water bottle and pressed it into the old man's hands. "Take it!" he said. "Old Surly will have fresh supplies on board. If you don't make it in another hour, we'll come back and fetch you!" With that, he set off, leaping down the remaining steps until he came to the last turning and saw the motor launch moored in a rocky inlet. Retreating into the shadowed part of the turning, which was barely visible from the beach, he saw two of the Prince's soldiers striding towards the motor launch. One of them grabbed Surly's arm. The other jabbed him with the butt of his rifle. He fell back against the side of his boat, shouting at his attackers. Then, he put a hand to his waist and pulled out a few coins from a wallet attached to his belt. The two soldiers seemed to be arguing with each other. Then the taller one that had hit him with the rifle butt reached over and pocketed the coins. The shorter one went on arguing. Surly shrugged and handed out a few more coins and they both nodded and moved away.

Josh smiled with relief.

But the men were heading for the steps! Josh could see from Surly's frantic movements that this was no part of his plan. He started towards them, then ran back to the boat, looked up at the steps and waved his hands in the air. He stood in doubt for a moment, then grabbed a knife from the motor launch, stuck it in his belt and hurried after them.

Josh couldn't afford to wait any longer. He raced back up the steps, eyes darting from side to side in search of a place to hide. He saw a few scattered bushes, then realised they were no use to him. He had to find Feathers first and search for a hiding place higher up the steps. With aching legs and a stitch in his side he kept going, counting the steps as he ran, "201, 202, 203..." He turned the corner and almost bumped into the old man, making his slow, painful backward descent. Feathers heard his cry and turned round. He listened as Josh spilled out his story in a rush.

"No time to hide," said Feathers, looking around him. "I can already hear them. Hm! They accepted money, eh? And Surly's coming this way. That may help." He sat down on the step. "I think we may be able to handle this," he said. "They don't know me, so I'm not very important to them but they've probably heard of you, so I suggest you lie flat under that bush." The bush provided scant cover but by edging around to the furthest point from the steps, Josh could listen and observe without being seen. Feathers had pulled out his pipe now and seemed comfortable with the notion of not having to move from that step. Josh peered further down. The soldiers were taking their time. He could hear them arguing about something. The taller one who had hit Surly with the rifle butt said, "Are you mad? We should have taken him back with us."

"But think about the money," said the other. "You accepted it. That's more than we earn in a month."

"Never mind the money. If the Prince finds out…"

"Never mind the money, he says! You took enough of it!"

"I took my share!"

"More than your share, I'd say…"

In a few more steps, they would round the bend and come face to face with Feathers. Surly had made good time. He was not far behind them. Feathers turned in Josh's direction and waved his pipe in the air. When he turned his head back to the steps, the two pirates were upon him.

"Nice evening," he said, in a booming, confident voice.

"What are you doing?" asked the taller soldier.

"Me? I live in these parts."

"No, you don't," said the shorter one.

"Well, maybe I don't, but I'm not doing anyone any harm."

"Get up!" said the taller one. "We're taking you to the Prince."

Feathers stayed seated. "In that case," he said "I might be forced to confess that I saw you accepting bribes. The Prince wouldn't like that."

"That settles it," said the taller one. "Let's shoot him."

"Far be it for me to advise you," said Feathers "but I wouldn't do that either. You might succeed but then I might get in first with this pistol. Besides, you'd have to hide my body somewhere, which is a lot of work in this heat for no reward. Is it worth it?"

There was a long silence, and then the shorter one turned to his colleague and said, "Let's go." The taller one nodded. "You can count yourself lucky!" he said, brushing past Feathers as he strode up the steps.

"I am indeed a lucky man," said Feathers, puffing on his pipe. He waved to Old Surly who moved up the steps to greet him as soon as the two soldiers rounded the bend out of sight. Josh ran over to join them and he and Old Surly helped Feathers down the remaining steps to the motor launch.

CHAPTER FIFTEEN

T hey reached Humphrey's Island at sunrise. Josh nudged the sleeping Feathers, grabbed their two rucksacks and stepped out onto the beach. Staring along the jagged coastline to his left, he could see the lights of the harbour town in the west. Feathers said the Prince would turn this town into his army base, letting his troops fan out over the whole island.

He watched Feathers climb out of the motor launch, rubbing his eyes and giving his arms a good stretch. Then he dipped his hands in the salt water and bathed his face. "That's better," he said, taking a long, hard look at his surroundings. "I feel ready to face the day now!"

Josh laughed and passed him a sandwich and a fresh bottle of water. Feathers took a swig of water and pulled out his map. "Flatstones," he said. "Got it? I marked it with a cross. And the Hall of Pings. It's here. Not so far away; a couple of miles maybe." He pointed out three black specks circling the harbour. "We can't leave the boat here for long," he said. "Those helicopters will soon leave their base and patrol the coast. "They don't know we're here yet, but let's not help them find out." He called across to Old Surly. "It's getting light," he said. "Time for you to make a move."

"I was waiting for you to wake up," Old Surly called back.

"Yes, yes, well…You should have woken me! If you go up east past that headland, you'll find the place I told you about." He went over to the motor launch and handed the map to Surly.

"We'll meet you at nightfall, if not before," he said. "Do you see where I've marked it? It's the ideal spot, well hidden by trees."

Surly nodded and climbed out of the motor launch, calling to Josh to help him push it off the shingles into clear water. Then he hauled himself aboard, gave a quick wave and steered it towards the headland.

Josh heaved his rucksack onto his back. "How far is it to the Hall of Pings?" he asked.

"Not far," said Feathers. "A couple of miles, perhaps. I think we can even get there without crossing any roads. It's mostly fields as far as I remember. Of course, the Hall won't be open yet. It probably won't open for another few hours. Unless you can think of another way of finding her…" He gave Josh a searching look.

Josh screwed up his eyes. He opened them again and grinned. He'd always known that this would be the easy bit. "She's heading for the Hall," he said, pointing across the fields.

"Well, if you're sure."

"Yes. Let's go!"

"Do you know where you're going?" Feathers asked him an hour later as they struggled through a gap in the hedge into the next field.

"Yes."

The fields stretched on and on. They had to stick to the hedgerows and seek the cover of trees whenever a helicopter flew overhead. The girl with the stone had no idea of the dangers. They had to get to her soon.

Suddenly, as they emerged from another hedgerow into an open meadow, Feathers whispered: "There she is! Tall, fair hair

– unmistakable in these parts – do you see her – over there by the gate?"

Josh stopped and pushed back his hair, damp with sweat. He pulled a towel from his rucksack and mopped his face. His clothes felt hot and sticky and his mouth felt dry and he didn't know what to say or do. This was the girl with the stone of love! He hadn't imagined her as a real person before. He hung back, trying to let Feathers get ahead of him.

"What are you waiting for, Josh?" whispered Feathers.

He hitched up his jeans. "Just a moment, I have to get my breath back."

His heart beat faster. She stood there by the fence in a green tee-shirt and jeans, her fair hair tossing in the wind, unaware of any danger.

Josh hurried down the grassy path until he was in calling distance. "Hi!"

She started at the sound of his voice. He was afraid she would panic. Instead, she threw up her hands and strolled towards him, laughing.

"Hi! You're Josh! I was expecting you. I thought–"

He felt his face tingle and go red.

She came closer and searched his face. "Are you all right?" she asked. "I've been so excited about seeing you."

"So have I. About seeing you, I mean."

"I'm glad you're here." She gave him a hug.

"I'm glad you're here too," he said. Straightaway he knew that, as speech-making efforts go, it wasn't his best. "Well, you live here," he added, "but you know what I mean."

"And you've come to take me away," Lucy reminded him.

She was teasing him now.

"Yes, I got that bit wrong too," he said.

"Who cares?" she said. She squeezed his arm, and he began to relax and feel happy. Yes, happy.

"This is Sir William Feathers," he explained. "You met him, remember? The explorer."

"The explorer. Yes, the explorer," repeated Lucy, as if he had said something important.

Feathers shook her hand. "We're here to whisk you away to a place of safety," said Feathers.

"Oh but you can't do that," protested Lucy, looking at him as if he meant to seize her on the spot. "You see, there's my mother."

Feathers nodded. "That's all right. She can come with us."

Feathers scanned the sky again and started to move, but Lucy touched him on the shoulder. "There's one more thing," she began, avoiding his eyes. "There's my dad. He's with a strange lady." She turned to Josh for support. "I think they were both heading for our house."

"The Cat Lady!"

"What's the matter? Do you know her?"

"I'm afraid so!"

Feathers interrupted them. "Better make this quick, eh? We're very exposed here. What else did you see?"

"I think she's looking for the Hall of Pings. She came on a motorbike. She's given my dad a circlet thing to wear. My dad seems very proud of it." She twisted her hands in discomfort.

"We're finished, then," said Feathers. "This Cat Lady will tell the soldiers and they'll be waiting for us, either at the Hall, or at her house…"

Josh shook his head. "Not her!" he said. "She'd never tell the soldiers. She wants all the glory for herself. She'll track us down or wait for us at the house."

"I hope you're right," said Feathers. "You must be. We can't stay here deciding. Let's go, then."

"Go where?" asked Lucy.

"To your house. It's no use looking for the Cat Lady. She'll find us."

Lucy looked at Josh with pleading eyes.

"He's right," he said. "Never mind if she's there. We'll have to face her at some point."

Lucy nodded. "My house is over there," she said, pointing.

She led them back the way she had come, through the gate and into the next field. Ahead of them, Josh could see the gleam of the main road leading to the Hall of Pings, but Lucy headed for the woods on the right. She stopped in the shadow of the trees, where a straggling barbed wire fence protected a marshy swamp scattered with willows and silver birch. She pointed to a gap in the barbed wire, concealed by two gorse bushes and led them down an overgrown, muddy path winding through the trees.

As they walked side by side behind Feathers, Lucy pushed something into Josh's hand.

"Take it," she said. "It's my stone. Don't say anything. Just take it!"

She gave a satisfied sigh when he placed the onyx stone, larger than his own, in an inner pocket sewn inside his jeans. In return, he showed her two stones on golden chains, one of which he placed around her neck and one around his own. "They're fakes," he whispered, "but very convincing. My stepdad made them for me."

"Hurry up, you two," said Feathers, turning around and glaring at them. "If you must stand around chatting, wait till we get to the house!"

At that moment, they heard the sound of trampling feet approaching from the main road.

Feathers sighed. "We're really in trouble now," he said. "We spent too long by that fence!" They know we're here. The whole area will be stirring with soldiers soon. Let's get deeper into the woods! Come on!" He broke into a shuffling run.

The footsteps came to a halt at the point where they'd entered the woods. Josh held his breath. He heard two soldiers muttering to each other, then the sounds of branches being pushed aside.

"Get down! Flat on the ground!" whispered Feathers, throwing himself headlong into a patch of tall reeds.

Heavy boots crashed around in the undergrowth. Josh looked at Lucy lying flat out in the reeds, her face spattered with mud.

"They could be in there somewhere," a voice called out from behind the two gorse bushes. "Can you see anything?"

The second voice came from a few feet away. Josh lay rigid. "There's a path. It's a bit overgrown. Do you think it's worth having a look?"

"Not while there's just the two of us. The rest of the company will be here soon. Then we can search the whole area thoroughly."

The sound of footsteps receded.

"Do we know who we're looking for?"

"Yes, they were spotted a few fields back. A boy and a girl and a bearded man who looks like a walrus."

Josh pointed at Sir William who lay sprawled in a damp patch of reeds and grinned. He could hear from the clunk of their heavy boots that the soldiers had returned to the main road.

Feathers started to edge forwards on hands and knees, and he and Lucy followed. "We have to get a move on," said Feathers. "They know we're around here somewhere. But be careful!" he added. "And, if the worst comes to the worst, and we end up getting caught, no heroics, please! Just give up the stones. That's all they're after."

Josh winked at Lucy.

"This one, you mean?" she enquired, smiling, pointing to the stone round her neck.

Feathers snorted. "Yes, of course. Your stone."

Josh smiled.

"It can't be much further now," said Feathers, stopping to take another swig of water. "It seems to be getting lighter."

The trees thinned out and they soon reached the end of the woods, with a view over open country. Josh realised that they'd travelled in a horseshoe and were scarcely a mile from the point where they'd started their journey. On his right, he could see the headland and, beyond that, just out of sight, must be the cove where their motor launch had landed.

"That way's hopeless!" Feathers announced. "It's too flat and open. They know we're in this area. They're bound to spot us."

"Is there any other way?" asked Josh

Lucy pointed to their right. "In that direction, the woods go down to the water's edge. We can get to my house that way. I've done it before."

"You mean follow the coast?" he asked. He stared at the sheer cliffs on the far side of a tiny harbour.

Lucy seemed to guess his thoughts. "I've been this way before. There are steps cut into those cliffs. It's easy. And the pine forest goes on for miles on the other side."

"What's that noise? Sh!" Josh thought he heard the distant tremor made by the trample of heavy boots. It came from the woods behind them. "Do you hear it?"

Feathers frowned. "If we're smart, we can cross that little harbour before they get here. Lucy, you know the way. You'd better go first."

Lucy hurried down the rocky slope, weaving in and out of the trees and boulders. Josh scrambled to keep up with her, while Feathers puffed and panted along behind. After a time, the sound of trampling boots faded away. Any noise they now made was drowned by the sound of waves crashing against the harbour wall below.

"Can you see anything yet?" called Feathers in a hoarse whisper.

Josh turned and saw him, stooped and red in the face, some distance behind. He clutched the trunk of a fir tree and struggled to get his breath back. "Don't mind me, young Josh," he panted. "I'll be fine."

Josh peered up at him. He didn't look fine. Lucy had almost reached the shoreline by now, but there was still time. He waited.

"Not much further now," he whispered as Feathers caught up with him.

"Thank God for that!"

Lucy crouched at a point where the trees ended, about fifty feet above the harbour. A narrow stretch of grey sand bordered by overhanging rocks led to a sheer cliff face on the other side.

"Let's risk it," said Feathers. "Going back isn't an option. I'll go first, this time, as I'm the only one carrying a firearm."

Josh could hear the enemy now. They had emerged from the woods high up above and were firing random shots across the marsh. He grinned at Lucy, who smiled back and grasped his hand to pull herself to her feet.

"Are you ready Josh?" Feathers felt his way down the rocks. Lucy went next and Josh followed.

He stepped down onto the hard sand. It was high tide and the sky was darkening. Just a narrow strip of harbour wall lay between them and the cliffs opposite. Feathers strode ahead and Lucy jogged along behind.

A sound like a burst tyre broke the silence.

It came from the rocks above.

Josh froze.

Then silence again.

He hurried on after the others.

A clatter of rifle fire broke the silence. Voices screamed from the darkness above: "Stop! Stay where you are! Stand!"

Then the night air erupted in howls and screams as an avalanche of heavy bodies tumbled all around them.

Hooded shadows danced around them, waving their rifles in the air emitting strange, excited shrieks of triumph. Josh felt a rifle butt jabbed into the small of his back. He stuck close to Lucy, shielding her from the bodies jostling them from all sides.

Two soldiers whispered to each other and grabbed hold of Lucy's arms.

"You! Where's the Prince's stone?"

"I can see the chain. She's got it round her neck!"

One of them shoved Josh aside. They pulled Lucy away.

"Don't worry," she whispered over her shoulder. "I can handle this. They're no worse than some of the boys I work with."

As if to prove her wrong, one soldier grabbed her hair from behind while another reached for the chain. "Careful!" shouted his mate. "Don't break it. The Prince wants it all in one piece!"

Josh watched the care with which the soldier pulled the chain over her head with the stone attached to it. Then a voice called out. "What about the boy? He's got a stone too!"

"I haven't got it with me!" he called out.

"He's lying!"

"Look! He's holding something in his pocket! Give it here."

With a brave show of reluctance, he handed over the stone.

Feathers patted him on the back. "Well done, my boy! Well done, Lucy. At the end of the day, it's freedom that matters most. It's not worth risking your life for two stones."

The pirates went silent. A tall, hooded figure, who'd been leaning against the rocks, strolled forwards and poked Feathers in the chest with his rifle butt. "Who said anything about freedom?" The other pirates hung back, in awe of their leader. He placed a hand on Feathers' chest and gave him a shove to prove his point. "Eh? Who said anything about freedom?"

Josh bit his lip. Until this older man appeared, things had been going their way.

"Are you in charge?" the man asked Feathers. "Come over here where I can see you!"

Feathers followed him a few feet away from the group. They stood talking for a while. The soldiers started talking among themselves. Josh could see them getting restive. They had their stones. They wanted to get away and claim their reward.

Josh noticed that the older man had gone quiet. The soldiers stopped talking too and looked in his direction.

"My pistol is pointed at his heart," Feathers called out. "If he moves, if any of you move, I will shoot and he will die. Suit yourselves. You've got your stones. I'll release him when you're safely out of my sight."

Their leader opened his mouth to protest, but when Feathers released the safety catch, he held up both hands and surrendered his rifle with a shrug. That was enough for his men. They hurried off in a chattering group.

When the soldiers had climbed some distance away, Feathers removed the pistol from the man's chest. "I'll let you join your friends now," he explained. "You'd better hurry or they might be tempted to take all the credit for those stones." The man needed no persuading.

Feathers took a last look round. "I think it's safe to continue now," he said. "Let's make a start on those steps."

"How did you know the stones were fake?" asked Josh. They were climbing now, and he could hear the bearded explorer panting behind him.

"I didn't!"

Josh's mouth fell open. "You mean you were willing to give them up just like that?"

"What other choice was there?"

"You could have bargained them against his life."

"It wouldn't have worked. Not in my estimation. Sorry, Josh. I wasn't prepared to risk our lives – especially two young lives – for two stones."

Josh thought about this. He wouldn't have sold their position so cheaply, but Feathers was right in his way. He had no way of knowing that Josh's life depended on his stone. Josh felt their reassuring warmth in his pocket. They were halfway up the steps now. He could see right across the harbour to the wooded cliffs on the other side.

"Keep your head down!" Feathers panted from below.

They'd been spotted by a small group of soldiers on the other side of the harbour. Josh thought he heard scattered shots, but they must have fallen short of their mark or buried themselves in the surrounding rocks.

The steps were built into the rock face, making the climb difficult. He was more worried in case other troops were waiting for them when they got to the top. Lucy was too far ahead to heed any warning. With aching muscles, he scrambled to catch up with her. "Stop!" he cried. "Be careful!" he panted.

He hurried after her as she rounded the top of the steps. A flat patch of open meadow lay between the cliff top and the shelter of the trees. Lucy waited at the top and Josh soon lay beside her. Next, Feather's bearded red face emerged out of nowhere like a swimmer's head from the sea, and Josh and Lucy each grabbed an arm and pulled him to safety.

"That's where I live," said Lucy, pointing across the meadow to the woods beyond.

CHAPTER SIXTEEN

"I t's not far now," Lucy whispered, as they entered the woods. "This used to be a big private estate once. The main house is just ahead."

She led them across the weathered stone foundations of an old manor house which stuck up through the weeds and long grass. They crossed what was once a lawn, down some crumbling brick steps, past a fish pond choked with rubbish and algae, through an avenue of tall elms, and then on downwards through a wilderness of willows and brambles, until they saw an old stone gatehouse, poking out through the trees.

Josh tugged at Feathers' jacket. "Wait," he whispered. He listened for the sound of footsteps or a snapping twig. But the broad smile on the face of the woman emerging from the gatehouse filled him with hope. So, the Cat Lady wasn't in the house…but, of course, she wouldn't be! She wanted him inside the house so that she could activate the circlet!

The woman had to be Lucy's mother – she had the same laughing eyes – but she was shorter by a head with yellow hair tied up in a bundle. She held out her arms to greet them, then cried, then embraced them, then started speaking very fast in a language that Josh and Feathers couldn't understand.

"She's excited," explained Lucy. "She is very happy to meet you. She knows where we are going and she is ready to come with us."

Lucy gestured towards the open door, but Josh didn't budge. "What about your dad?" he asked.

"He's here! He's inside. My mum is so happy! Come on!"

"Don't go in!" Josh shouted. "Stop, Feathers. Move away. That's her plan – to get us all inside." He reached in his trousers and pressed the two stones into Lucy's hands. "Take these!" he cried, "and stand further back! And you, Feathers! Believe me! You have to go further than that!"

"Are you sure you know what you're doing?" asked Feathers, unwilling to make a move. "Can't you use your stone?"

"No need," said Josh. "I know where the Cat Lady is. She's out there somewhere, watching us, waiting to explode the circlet."

"But as soon as you get inside, it will go off."

"Not if I'm quick. I promise!"

Feathers grunted and turned his heavy frame around, urging Lucy and her mother to get back.

Josh waited until they had reached a safe distance from the house, then stepped inside and found the old tribesman sitting alone in a bare, whitewashed room, smiling and fingering the circlet round his neck. As the old man rose from his chair to greet him, Josh whipped out the tool that Sandy had given him and pointed it at the circlet. With the glitter of a tiny screw speeding through the air, the device round the old man's neck sprang apart.

The old man just sat there, angry and confused. He looked down at the gift hanging round his neck, broken and useless.

Josh hurried to the door. "It's safe to come in now!" he cried.

"My dad?" asked Lucy, leading her bewildered mother back into the house.

"Yes, he's safe. I've broken his circlet. I think he's angry with me. Maybe you could explain."

"Explain?"

"The circlet had a bomb. It's safe now."

"You saved him!"

Lucy's mother just stood there looking confused. Lucy put an arm over her shoulder and drew her into the gatehouse, chattering away again in a strange language.

Feathers stooped as he entered. His large presence filled the room. "What did you do?" he asked Josh.

"I'll explain later."

"But what about Miss Cattermole?"

"She's around here somewhere, but not too close. She's waiting for that thing to go off." Josh grinned. "She likes spectacles. Don't you remember?" he asked.

Feathers patted him on the back. "I'll say this for you, young Josh," he said. "You acted quickly there. You saved us all!"

"I knew what she'd do. That's all."

"And what will she do now?"

Josh went to the window and scanned the woods behind. "She must be out there somewhere," he said, "where she can see us but we can't see her. She's waiting for a loud bang."

"Won't she realize that the device isn't working?"

"I don't think she's tested it yet. She needed all of us to step inside. She couldn't risk leaving one of us alive to walk off with those stones." He turned to Lucy. "Maybe you could persuade your dad to part with that circlet?"

Lucy held it above her head. The old tribesman was smiling now, revealing a few yellowing teeth. "I've explained what you did," she said. "He thinks you're a warrior now." She passed him the circlet. "What are you going to do?" she asked.

"I'm going to attract the cat!"

He bent over in the doorway and fiddled with Sandy's tool, then stepped a few paces outside and lobbed the reactivated circlet into the undergrowth. "Let's see if she comes," he said, as he re-entered the room.

The five of them sat around on the floor with their backs to the wall and waited. Lucy and her family didn't know what to expect and soon broke into a whispered conversation. Josh heard his name mentioned several times and the old tribesman pointed at him and showed Lucy a small leather sack. Lucy looked inside it and shuddered and giggled a bit, from which Josh guessed that the sack contained presents for himself that might not be to everyone's taste. Then the mother looked inside the sack and took a sideways look at Josh and laughed and shook her head.

Feathers frowned and said 'Sh!" and put his fingers to his ears and Lucy and her family did the same. Then they all heard it. It could hardly be called a bang because the noise was muffled by the undergrowth but they all heard a distinct 'phut'.

Josh shrugged. How would the Cat Lady react? Would she realize that her plan hadn't worked? Or was she too far away to gauge the effect of her 'bomb'? Surely she'd want to find out? He imagined her peering through the window. Should he close it so that she couldn't see in? No, she'd notice the change. "Keep away from the window!" he warned. "She's on her way! Stand flat against the wall where she can't see you!"

Everyone sat or stood in the darkened corners of the room and waited. Josh looked at his watch. A full five minutes went by. He thought for one moment that he saw an inquisitive face staring through the window, but the vision passed, and he didn't know if he'd imagined it. Then Feathers coughed and everyone started. And then, just as he was becoming despondent, he heard a light tapping on the door.

"Come in!" said Feathers. "Please don't be shy! We've been expecting you!"

Josh smiled to himself. Catherine Cattermole, the Cat Lady, was never shy! And embarrassment or shame stood way beyond her reach. She took in the situation at a glance and stepped lightly into the room, wishing everyone well as if she'd quite forgotten that she had just tried to kill them. Feathers went red in the face with moral indignation but, as Josh knew, he needn't have bothered. He was talking to a cat. The Cat Lady listened politely enough, but then she explained that she was only trying to carry out her master's commands. "So you've failed him," said Feathers, somewhat harshly. "What do you think he'll do now?"

Even Josh found her reaction hard to believe. Had she really not thought about this before? She seemed to live entirely in the present, moving from one emotion to another like someone walking from one room to the next, slamming doors. Now she sat, huddled up on a chair, and sobbed and sobbed. She fingered the circlet round her neck and said "He'll kill me. I know it."

"Maybe I can help," said Josh.

Her head lifted a little and her eyes peeped out from her hands. "Can you really help me? Oh, please, please help me," she said.

"Well, I can undo that circlet thing."

"Can you really? Oh, please, please undo it!"

"But not now, because you'd betray us."

"I would never betray you, Josh. How could I betray you?"

"You'd run off and tell those soldiers who've been hunting us."

Josh saw from the flicker in her eyes that he'd just given her a good idea. "But you won't do that," he said, "because I won't release you until we're halfway to Amaryllis."

"So I hope you can swim," said Feathers. His eyes brightened at the prospect.

The Cat Lady turned to Josh as her only hope. "You wouldn't do that, would you Josh? You wouldn't leave me to drown?"

Josh stood up. "No, we won't drown you," he said. "We'll drop you off on an island and then I'll undo your circlet. Let's go and find that boat."

Lucy's mother looked from one speaker to the other, struggling to grasp what was going on. Lucy threw an arm over her shoulder and whispered a few words in her ear. Her mother nodded and ran up the stairs, returning with a few belongings shoved into a leather sack which she carried over her shoulder. She nodded again to show that she was ready to set off.

"It's hard leaving so much behind," said Lucy, "but I explained it to her. She understands."

Her mother gave an uncertain smile, trying to read their meaning from their faces.

Feathers looked at his watch. "It's about half a mile to the motor launch," he said. "Let's go. You took a risk," he said to Josh, as he led them out of the house, "but your plan worked. And as for this charming lady–" he eyed the Cat Lady with disgust – "I suppose it's a good idea to take her with us, but we can always blow her up or drown her if she steps out of line."

CHAPTER SEVENTEEN

"The Prince is in the news again," said Feathers, slamming down a copy of *The Daily Trumpeter* on the kitchen table. "What does his lordship want for breakfast?"

"Bacon and eggs?" suggested Josh, pushing his luck. He wasn't used to having breakfast served to him like this.

"Very well, then. Bacon and eggs it shall be."

This was their third day in Feathers' rented bungalow overlooking Fortuna Harbour. They'd released the desperate Cat Lady on the nearest small island and taken the direct route for Amaryllis, arriving a few days before the ship. Lucy and her family had their own three-bedroom house on the hilly outskirts of town, donated by the Pirate Council as a reward for bringing the lost stone of love home to Amaryllis.

Josh grabbed the newspaper and read out the headline. "'Prince offers reward for missing stone'." What does that mean?"

"It means he hasn't got the stone of knowledge," said Feathers, wiping his hands on his apron and handing Josh his breakfast.

"Yes, but why does he want that stone and not the other two?"

"Because he knows where to find them," said Feathers. "Look on the bright side. He hasn't got it yet. You're safe for the moment."

Josh sat and stared at the front page. He'd been so occupied with the stone of love that he'd pushed that other stone to the back of his mind. Didn't his dad promise to post him a list of people who'd visited the museum on the day the stone was stolen? His letter should have arrived by now. His thoughts were interrupted by the sound of the doorbell. "I'll get it," he said, laying the paper aside. "That'll be Lucy."

"Clever girl," said Feathers. "She's getting to know what sort of time you get up; eleven o' clock on the dot."

Josh grinned. On the past two mornings he'd been in bed when Lucy called. His spirits lightened as he opened the door.

He found himself staring at the smiling, inquisitive face of Frederic Forbes.

"Oh, Mr Forbes. You're early! Where are the others?"

Frederic Forbes rubbed his hands in pleasant anticipation. "The ship has just docked. Do you mind if I come in? Bosworthy has gone off to find lodgings. I made my own arrangements long in advance through a cousin of mine who lives in Amaryllis, so I thought I would come here straightaway. Where are the other young people?"

"Sandy and Megs went down to harbour to see you lot arrive."

"Oh dear! What a pity I missed them." Frederic Forbes was already shaking hands with Feathers, who took off his apron and came and sat beside him on the sofa in the lounge. "I just couldn't wait to hear all your news," he continued, "and to meet the girl with the stone."

"Lucy," put in Josh.

"Yes, Lucy – and the captain and Jenkins too – I thought I heard that they'd been released…?"

"They're on their way. But they had to stop off on Elephant Island first," explained Feathers.

"Oh dear, yes. Well, business calls, I suppose." He sat back with a sigh of contentment. "I must say it has always been my ambition to travel to Amaryllis."

"Have you seen the news?" asked Feathers. "The Prince is offering a reward for the stone of knowledge."

"Oh yes, I noticed that. That was in *The Daily Trumpeter*, wasn't it? Mind you, I never believe half of what they write in that wretched rag."

The door rang again. This time it was Lucy. "I've just seen the pirate ship," she explained to Josh, as she burst into the room. "It's attracted quite a crowd down at the harbour. That's what kept me." She turned and noticed Frederic Forbes. He greeted her with little murmurs of delight, quizzing her about her family and her life in Humphrey's Island and her miraculous escape to Amaryllis.

Josh went to the window and scanned the harbour. He was thinking about the stone of knowledge and wondering if he could find it and deliver the restored necklace to the Temple of Harmony. But the thief was still out there somewhere. His stepdad's letter might hold the vital clue. It could be waiting for him at the post office. Why hadn't he thought of that?

This time the door rang twice, two loud rings. That had to be Megs! She didn't wait for an answer but rushed in, dragging John Bosworthy with her. "I met him at the harbour," she said. "He was about to wander off before I grabbed him and brought him here."

Bosworthy blinked and smiled. "I was going to look for lodgings," he said.

Everyone got to their feet and excited greetings echoed round the room.

"Where's Gregory?" asked Josh.

"He's with Sandy," said Megs, standing in the centre of the room and looking around her. "Gregory's gone a bit lame in one leg. Sandy is helping him."

"Shall we go and find them?" Josh whispered to Megs. He was already making for the door. "I thought we might see round the town, just the four of us," he suggested.

"Good idea!" said Megs, "I want to do some serious shopping. She held out her purse crammed full of screwed-up notes. "Look! I'm loaded! Your mum gave me all this money at the start of our journey and I never got the chance to spend it. You can have some if you like."

"I'm fine, thanks."

"Well, you know what I'm going to do?" She did a little jig. "I'm going to shop, shop, shop, shop till I drop!"

She turned and noticed Sandy standing outside the garden gate. "Hi, Sandy!" she cried. "We were just going out. I thought we could do some shopping," she added.

"Oh. Do we have to?"

Gregory stopped and opened a weary eye, saying in a low tigerish murmur, "That's what humans like to do when they are not busy killing each other. I suppose it's a harmless occupation."

"What's he saying?" Sandy asked

Megs rushed up and hugged the tiger, tickling the folds in his neck. "He says it's a good idea," she said. "But I think we should take him inside and make him comfortable first."

Josh led them back inside the bungalow, where Gregory discovered Lucy and basked in her admiration for a while before limping over to the fireplace and falling asleep.

"It may be a bit of a problem," Bosworthy whispered, "finding somewhere for him to stay."

"He could stay here, couldn't he?" Josh asked Feathers.

"Or at our house!" suggested Lucy. "I'd love him to stay at our house."

Josh thought of Lucy's house stuck away up a hillside. Gregory would make sure she was safe. He gave an eager nod.

"Good. That's settled then," said Lucy. "Now, I've got something to show you." She emptied the contents of a small snakeskin bag on the table. "I'm sorry about this," she began.

"But my dad insisted. It's a present for Josh. Maybe you could just keep it somewhere safe and bring it out next time my dad comes round."

Everyone leaned over the table.

"What's this?" asked Josh, pulling a necklace out of the bag.

"It's a necklace," said Lucy, blushing.

"I can see it's a necklace, but what are the beads made of?"

"Teeth."

"They look almost human."

"Put it away. It's not important."

"And what's this? It's very well wrapped up."

Lucy inspected it and quickly handed it back. "Don't remove the wrapping or it will smell the house out," she said. "That's yuck dung."

"I could have done with that thirty years ago," mused Feathers, "when my mother-in-law was around." He patted Lucy on the shoulder. "Only joking!"

The last object was an old tobacco tin with holes in the lid.

"If that's what I think it is," said Frederic Forbes, eyes glistening with interest, "I wouldn't advise you to open it. It's a poisonous toad. Dead, I assume, but that doesn't affect its deadly venom. Toads like that are an endangered species. The old man must think very highly of you, Josh. These objects are greatly valued on Humphrey's Island."

"Thanks," said Josh uncertainly. "I mean, thank your dad from me. I'll just put it away in my bedroom for the moment." He turned to Feathers. "We were thinking of making a short trip to town, just the four of us."

"Good."

"I need to stop off at the post office. There may be a letter from my stepdad."

"Good idea. Except it's closed. It's Sunday, remember."

"Oh."

He closed the door behind him and followed his friends down the hill to the quayside. Normally this was his favourite place. He enjoyed hearing the cries of fishermen and street vendors. And he liked watching the sailors swarming up the masts of the pirate ships with their crimson sails rocking in the bay. Their own ship stood proudly among them, attracting a crowd of onlookers.

Sandy and Megs hurried on ahead, walking in and out of the shops. Josh lagged behind with Lucy, lost in his own thoughts. They still had to find that stone. Maybe there was another way. He stopped outside an open-air café.

"Lucy?" he asked.

"Yes?"

"You know when we first met? I knew where to find you through my stone."

Her eyes glowed. "That was amazing."

"Yes, but my point is – couldn't we use the same method to find the third stone?"

She looked doubtful. "To me it's just a stone. You're different. Maybe you could try it?"

"Let's sit down for a moment. Don't let other people see what I'm doing."

"What about Sandy and Megs?"

"They'll find us."

He placed the two stones on the table and compared them. The larger stone of love looked altogether darker and richer than his own. He picked up his stone of truth which was so familiar to him in his left hand and the other stone in his right. A strange tingling sensation ran through his veins, stronger than anything he'd experienced before.

"Did you know," he asked Lucy, "that the Guardian, Matilda, created these stones as a cure for epilepsy?"

"Ye-es," said Lucy uncertainly. "You have epilepsy, don't you?"

"I had it worse when I was younger. I use my stone to control it."

"And the stone that used to be mine – does that help?"

"It seems to. I can see things much more clearly with your stone."

He closed his eyes.

"Can you see anything now?"

"That stone's here in Amaryllis," he said. "I know that for sure."

"Can you see all that from those stones?"

He opened his eyes and blinked in the bright midday sunlight. "I don't know," he said. "I suppose so. For a moment, I just had a very clear picture of a desk beneath the window in a small attic bedroom overlooking the sea. Some sort of guesthouse, I suppose."

"What else did you see?"

"A single bed, a chair, and a desk. The ring lay in a silver dish on the desktop."

Josh felt a felt a prickly sensation at the back of his neck. Somewhere in Amaryllis was a person who'd stolen the stone from the museum and had probably picked up the newspaper and was looking for the Prince's reward. What if he was after the other stones too? That would deserve an even greater reward. He and this unknown person were tiptoeing in the dark, hunting each other.

The waitress stood at their table. "Are you ready to order?"

"No, we're all right thanks," said Josh, standing up. He pulled Lucy out of her chair and pointed down the street. "Look! There's Megs," he said. "Sandy's lagging behind as usual. Hi, Megs!" he said, as soon as she got within speaking distance. "I've found out about that stone. It's here in Amaryllis."

"Can you be more specific?" asked Sandy. Josh could see from his expression that following Megs round the shops had dented his enthusiasm. "I mean it's like saying you've just found a needle and it's somewhere in a haystack."

"Well, it's in a small attic room overlooking the harbour. Is that better?"

"It could be a guesthouse," said Sandy – "or a guest room. I mean people with large houses don't usually sleep in the attic." He pointed at the rooftops overlooking the harbour. "But all these houses have attics," he added.

"I know a place that might help," said Megs. "It's really cool! It's called the Cave of Prophecy."

"How can prophecies help us find a stone?" asked Sandy.

Megs shrugged. "Maybe they can prophesy where the stone can be found?" she suggested. "We can ask Sybil."

"Don't you mean the Sybil? asked Josh.

"No, what's that? She's a fat lady called Sybil. She told my fortune, and she got most of it right."

"It's worth a try, I suppose," said Josh. "Is it far from here?"

"No. It's just up there."

'Up there' meant a bumpy ride up the mountain in a green open-top bus that poured out a trail of black smoke as it rattled and groaned round precarious hairpin bends. They stepped out onto a dusty square surrounded by brightly painted tourist kiosks selling sweets and souvenirs.

"The Cave of Prophecy is over there," said Megs, pointing at a straight path made of small, square stones and bordered by cypresses, which led up the mountain. "The cave's not far ahead but if you go right to the end, you will come to the Temple of Harmony."

The cave itself didn't look promising. There were no other visitors. All they saw was a fat gipsy lady sitting behind a rickety table at the entrance to an artificial grotto. She beckoned them towards her. "Fortunes or prophecies?" she asked in a harsh, business-like voice.

"Both, in a way," said Josh.

"Well, make up your mind. If it's both, I'll have to charge double!"

"Let's start with fortunes," suggested Megs.

"That'll cost you ten Esmeraldas."

"Ten!" protested Megs. "That's a rip-off!"

The fat lady threw back her head and glared. "Careful! You've offended the spirits."

Megs looked in her bag and handed over a screwed-up note. "How are the spirits now?" she asked. "Happier?"

"Much happier," the lady agreed. "Now, how can I help you?"

"We are looking for the stone of knowledge," Josh explained.

"Ah yes, a very important stone, that. You'll have to wait while I go into my trance."

The fat lady shut her eyes and panted and wobbled around for a bit on her chair, sweat forming on her broad forehead and down the folds of her chin.

"This is a waste of time," whispered Josh.

"I know," whispered Megs. "Last time it was different. I suppose I was younger."

Just then, the lady jerked upright and opened her eyes. "I have communed with the spirits," she said, "and they have told me the stone of knowledge is a very valuable stone and—"

"Yes, but what did they tell you?" asked Megs.

"It'll cost you another ten Esmeraldas. That's what they said," the lady explained.

"Forget it! Just walk away!" whispered Josh, starting to walk off.

"I'll give you two," said Megs.

"The spirits won't be happy with two," said the lady.

"That's all they're getting," said Megs.

The lady sighed and was about to go into another trance but thought better of it. "Oh, very well then, two," she agreed, snatching the offered coins.

"Go on, then," said Megs. "What did the spirits tell you?"

"It's a very important stone," said the lady, looking at them very hard. "Where did you lose it?"

"We didn't lose it!" exclaimed Josh. "We never had it!"

"Ah! So it's not yours, then. You see I need to know these things in order to interpret the signs correctly." She went into another trance, a shorter one. As she explained, she didn't do longer trances for two Esmeraldas

"Look! This is hopeless," said Megs. "Just tell us what the spirits say and we'll go."

The lady fixed her dark eyes on Megs face. "The spirits say," she began, waggling a pudgy finger in Megs' face, "they are very insistent on this point. They say to keep looking because it must be somewhere. That's what they say."

"That's it?" shouted Megs. "It must be somewhere?"

"That's what they say," said the lady. "Don't shoot the messenger. But if I was you," she added, "seeing as I want to help you, I'd look for someone who's after your other stones. So he or she – it could be a she – must know a little bit about you."

They took the bus down the hill, laughing but dispirited. Once they all understood that there was someone out there in Amaryllis who not only possessed the stone of knowledge but probably had designs on the other stones too, they went quiet for the rest of the journey.

The sun was beginning to set when they arrived back at the bungalow. Feathers was alone in the kitchen preparing the evening meal. He handed Sandy a map which John Bosworthy had drawn for him, showing him the way to his lodgings. Gregory rose to his feet and accompanied Lucy back to her house in the hills, and only Josh and Megs were left, facing Feathers across the kitchen table.

"Never mind, my boy," said Feathers. "You'll just have to go the post office first thing in the morning. That means getting up early. Do you think you can manage that?"

Josh grinned. "Did the others stay long?" he asked.

"Oh yes. Chatting away. Frederic Forbes was most impressed by this place, by the way. He seemed to think the rent rather reasonable. He insisted on having a good look round. According to Forbes, the house is quite old; two hundred years, at least. He should know, I suppose."

"What's that noise?" asked Josh. He looked at Megs, who nodded. They had both heard a double tap on the French windows leading into the garden.

"Can you see who it is?" asked Feathers. "I'll just get these plates onto the table."

Megs got up to help with the dishes, while Josh walked into the lounge and peered through the frosted glass. He could just make out the empty patio and the lawn beyond.

A pebble hit the window.

"What was that?" called Feathers. "Can you see anything?"

"Someone's out there," said Josh. "I'll go and check."

As he stepped outside, he could hear Feathers calling "Wait for me! I'm coming with you."

But he was already standing on the empty lawn, letting his eyes grow attuned to the dark. He stepped across the grass towards the white fence bordering the lawn.

That's when they grabbed him. His face hit the lawn with sickening force and a heavy body landed on his back, reaching a sweating arm round his neck. He struggled to free himself, but the needle thrust into his arm weakened his resistance.

"I've got him. Get the stones!"

"They're not round his neck!"

"Try his pockets!"

"Hoy!" The last voice from far away sounded like Feathers.

He felt a lightness in his pocket as the stones were lifted away but his feeble protests were muffled in the grass. The needle was beginning to take effect. He felt himself falling into the peaceful darkness of oblivion, punctuated by pistol shots from the world he had just left.

CHAPTER EIGHTEEN

Josh's mind swam like a fish in a glass tank, unable to reach events in another world. He felt the sofa beneath him, his head on Megs' lap. He smelt the enamel bowl on the floor at Megs' feet, but everything seemed far away.

Someone shook him. "Wake up, Josh." It was Megs. He knew she was there, but he couldn't get to her.

He heard a door bang and heavy footsteps approaching the sofa. "I shot one of them." That was Feathers. "I shot him in the leg. He was trying to make off with the stones."

He felt a hand pressing the stones into his hand. That was Megs. He couldn't hold them. The stones dropped to the floor. He felt himself sinking.

"Come on, Josh," said the voice. "Do your best." The stones were in his hand again and he felt Megs' hand pressing his fingers round it. A weak surge of power returned to his fingers. He wanted to vomit, but the sweet world of oblivion beckoned and he floated away.

Voices tugged at his consciousness from the world he'd just left.

"Phone the hospital." That was Megs.

"Yes, the hospital. And the police…a wounded man… need to question him."

"The hospital!" Her voice rang in his ears.

"Got to find him…The man I shot."

"Why?"

"…don't know what was in that poison…ring the hospital… the police…give him water and help him to sick up…"

"And blankets?"

"Yes, blankets…"

The sweet world beckoned. Warm blankets covered him, but he still felt cold. He heard Feathers on the phone. His voice sounded loud. "I need to know what to give him," he said. "I didn't say 'swallowed'…I said 'injected'! Of course, I'm keeping him warm! So you keep saying! It's been ten minutes!"

Megs stroked the stone in the palm of his hand. He tried to touch her hand with his fingers, to make contact with that world he had left.

He heard the door open and heavy footsteps enter the room.

"Are you Sir William Feathers? How do you spell that name, sir?"

"I don't! I've got a sick boy on my hands. He's been poisoned and I need to know what substance he's swallowed."

The sick boy was him! He saw the sick boy lying on the couch. The policeman was talking.

"All in good time, sir."

Feathers was shouting. "There isn't any time, my good fellow. Someone has injected poison into his veins. And we need to know the kind of poison he used. I want you to find that man. He can't have gone far. I should know, because I shot him in the leg."

"You did what, sir?"

"You heard me!"

"There's no need to take that tone with me, sir. And if it's the person I'm thinking of, he's not going to be much use to us, because that person is already dead."

"Not by me he isn't! I told you I shot him in the leg."

"So you say sir," responded the voice, "You can explain all that down at the police station."

The voices left the room like a train hurrying on to the next station. New voices arrived.

He heard whispers, from Megs, whose strong arms supported his shoulders, and from two women holding him up on either side. They jostled him onto a kind of bed, sending shockwaves through his stomach until his mind roared down a dark tunnel into oblivion.

He opened his eyes. He lay in a hospital bed. An old man in a white coat poked and prodded him with gleaming silver instruments, but he couldn't feel anything; just a flicker of life in his hands, which were clutching two stones. Lucy sat beside him now. He opened his mouth to speak to her, but the words wouldn't come. She pressed his hand, and he moved his eyes a little in her direction. The stones felt like an unseen source of energy, but far, far away. He heard what was going on around him but couldn't take part.

"Before we proceed any further," the doctor was saying, "I will need details of his next of kin."

"I'll deal with all that!" said a new voice. That was Feathers.

"Are you his grandfather?"

He couldn't remember if Feathers was his grandfather. He was talking about the poison.

"Unfortunately, the two persons who injected it couldn't help me. They were found lying in a side street not far from my bungalow, with their throats slashed."

Feathers's face loomed over him. "So how are we doing?"

He felt the grip of Lucy's hand and tried to respond to Feathers' question with a blink of the eyes. He heard the doctor saying. "It's not looking good. Unless we can find the source of these toxins they've pumped into his body…"

Feathers' face swam away again. He was talking to someone. "Have you tried antidotes for snake bite? That sort of thing?"

"We have tried every obvious local poison that corresponds with his symptoms. We have cures for most of those, if there are cures. It would help if we knew where this poison originated."

"Humphrey's Island or Windfree."

Josh knew this was important. He struggled to get back to that distant world. He tried to tighten his hold on the stones. Another flicker of life. He opened his mouth. They were watching him now. He felt Lucy's arms around him and her eyes willing him to speak. "The t…" he started, "The to–"

Her bright eyes absorbed his meaning. "The toad!" she cried, "the poisonous toad!"

Josh closed his eyes. It was so deliciously peaceful in his warm bed.

Feathers was still speaking. "Spindlefroth," he said. "…juice they extract from the bark of the Spindlewood tree."

"Not much use to us." That was the doctor… "going to Humphrey's Island looking for tree bark."

"Buy the stuff in an Art shop… mix it with white spirit…. buy it in its pure form...How is the patient now?"

They were talking about him!

"He's hanging in there, but not for much longer, unless this liquid does the trick."

He heard a door bang. Feathers had gone. He tried to remember why. Lucy still had her arms round him. He had to stay awake because that's what her arms were asking him to do.

He could hear the doctor tapping away at a computer in another part of the room. "Slipodyxia," he was saying, "Smidge Bite...Spindlefroth…an all-purpose remedy used by the natives on Humphrey's Island as an antidote for poisons ranging from snake bite to toad venom."

He felt Lucy's stone pressing into his hand. Her face was very close to him. He wanted to respond for her sake but felt his energy slipping away. The doctor was speaking again…

"Nurse Dawkins, can you go down to the canteen and fetch me a pint of milk?"

The voice of Feathers again. "I've got it!"

Sudden footsteps, whispers and the clink of instruments, shadows hovering over the bed.

"Hold his head up, young lady. That's right. Nurse Dawkins, undo the cap for me, can you? I can't get it open. Good girl. Now pour two spoonfuls into the milk. Stir it well. We've got to get his mouth open. I'll stick a spoon down his throat. Good. Now, pour in the liquid – all of it – and prepare some more just in case."

His head felt as if it was going to crack with pain. A volcano in his stomach dragged up its molten fluids to the point of eruption and then stuck there, pressing more pain into his head. Far away, the doctor sounded excited. "Something's happening…Can you hold him up a bit, young lady? Well done! He's showing signs of life. Watch it! He'll be sick all over you if you're not careful."

And then, whoosh! And again, whoosh! He was sick again and again. Finally, the pain in his head had gone. He lay back, exhausted but alive.

He looked at Lucy. Her face and clothes were a mess, but her eyes were radiant.

"Sorry," he said. He could speak! He could move his fingers.

She squeezed his hand. It felt good.

"That's not the end of it," warned the specialist.

He was able to turn his head and observe the man in the white coat speaking to the nurse.

"Let's get some more of that liquid down him. Plenty of milk in the mixture this time; it will help him get rid of the rest of it."

Feathers came over and patted him on the shoulder. "Well done, Josh. I'll be back in a bit." Lucy still sat by his side. He could relax and go to sleep; a long, deep, dreamless sleep.

It was full daylight when he woke to the sound of a slamming door. Feathers had entered the room. A look of momentary annoyance crossed his face. "Where's Lucy?" he asked.

Lucy came running in and took her place on the bedside chair. She took Josh's hand. "I've just had a shower," she said. "Where's Forbes?"

Feathers looked around, as if expecting Frederic Forbes to emerge from some corner of the room.

"He offered to come and sit with Josh while I went to the bathroom," Lucy explained. "I don't understand it. He promised to stay." She gripped Josh's hand. "I would never have left you alone."

"Lucy's been here all night," Feathers assured him.

"Megs too!" Lucy reminded him.

"Yes, they've taken shifts. And Gregory has been allowed to sleep outside your door."

Josh felt vaguely uneasy. Did that mean he was in danger?

"I've brought you a letter from your stepdad," said Feathers, handing him a bulky envelope.

"Thanks."

Lucy raised his head and pushed another pillow under it so that he could see to read.

"Thanks." He had already torn the letter open and his eyes raced down the first page.

"My parents are arriving tomorrow," he said.

"That's great," whispered Lucy.

He was already on the next page. "No!" He cried. "No, I can't believe it!"

"What's up?" asked Feathers.

"You know I mentioned a bomb that went off on Discovery Island. The man that was killed was Frederic Forbes!"

"No!" exclaimed Feathers.

"But how can that be? I mean you knew him! You'd already met him."

"I knew of him," agreed Feathers. "I never met him. Then who is that man we thought we knew? He seemed such a decent fellow. I can't believe…What does your stepdad say in the rest of the letter?"

"It doesn't matter, does it?" said Josh, putting the letter down. "He's given me a list of names of the people who visited the museum on that day but the man we know as Frederic Forbes won't be among them because that's not his real name."

"And that man was alone with you just now!" exclaimed Feathers. "Feel under your pillow! Josh! Lucy!"

Josh knew immediately what he wouldn't find. The two stones had gone.

"I only left the room a few minutes ago!" cried Lucy. "He can't be far away."

"We must check the harbour and airports," said Feathers.

"But where would he go?" asked Josh. "Windfree?"

"Probably. If he's stupid. He's more likely to end up dead like those two pirates that attacked you!"

Josh struggled to understand where Feathers' thoughts were leading him. "Why dead?"

"The stone of knowledge is one thing. The Prince would pay good money for it. But if this man's got the whole necklace, killing him is the better option. He doesn't want him hanging out for a better price – far easier to have him killed. We have to act fast."

"Gregory!" exclaimed Josh. "Where's Gregory?"

"Why Gregory?" asked Feathers.

"Tigers have a strong sense of smell. If he hasn't gone far, Gregory can track him down."

Feathers shrugged. "We have to try everything, I suppose." He strode around the room, banging his fist into the palm of his other hand. "Harbour and airports, the police. I have to get to the phone."

Lucy had already slipped out of the room to speak to Gregory.

Feathers was still dithering, muttering to himself. "To think I let that man wander around the bungalow. Just wait till I get hold of him! Just wait!" He strode out of the room.

Josh struggled to raise himself from the bed. It was no use. He didn't have the strength. He wanted to cry.

Megs rushed into the room. "Hi, Josh! You look better!"

"They've taken the stones!"

"I know, but you look better! That's what matters!"

"Where's Lucy?"

"She's gone with Gregory. She asked me to take her place. Sandy's around too. He's gone to check out Frederic's lodgings; the man who called himself Frederic. Don't worry. He can't have gone far." She put an arm round Josh's shoulder. "You're going to get better. That's all we care about."

The sound of an ambulance echoed from the street below. Then more ambulances, and police cars, sirens blaring. Megs rushed to the window. "There's a crowd gathering at the end of the street!" she cried. "The ambulances are stopping. It's a long way away and the people are blocking my view but they are surrounding someone who's lying on the ground. Let's hope it's Frederic Forbes."

She came and sat beside Josh again and he showed her the letter from his parents. Anything to pass the time!

"I wonder what his real name is?" she asked. "There's fifty names on this list."

Josh's eyes rested on the name 'Frederic Fraterno'. "That's the one," he said.

"Frederic Fraterno? Why are you so sure?"

"Because he mentioned that family but he never mentioned anyone of that name. Besides..."

"Besides what?"

"They are related to the family who originally stole the Prince's stone."

"Related to Lucy, you mean?"

"I'm afraid so. It doesn't mean anything, but she'll be gutted when she finds out."

Feathers strode into the room. His face looked flushed and animated. "He did it!" he cried. "Gregory got his man! I don't know what happened to that limp. I'd no idea he could go at that speed. He caught him up before he reached the end of the street."

"What are you hiding behind your back?" asked Megs.

Feathers grinned and opened his hairy fist. "Just a few stones. Three of them!"

CHAPTER NINETEEN

"**G**o on, Josh, put it on!" said Josh's mum. "The girls went all the way to the monastery to collect it from that awful priestess. You have to wear it!" The two girls on the sofa rocked with laughter.

Josh's parents had stayed for a week, taking over the bungalow to nurse him through his illness. Feathers had found a bachelor pad for himself, overlooking the harbour. He told Josh that the swap suited him because Josh's mum insisted on cooking all his meals at the house. Besides, he could have long conversations with Josh's stepdad, sitting in the garden, smoking his pipe, with a glass of wine in his hand. John Bosworthy joined them on most days. Josh didn't know what they found to talk about, but the Prince got mentioned frequently, as did Magnus Maxtrader and, of course, the man calling himself Frederic Forbes.

This was the day Josh had to make the trip to the Temple of Harmony with crowds lining the route and the Maxtrader press filming the ceremony. But that was later. He was feeling in fine form again and in no mood to be bullied into putting on a fancy costume, with the two girls and Sandy sitting on the sofa, making fun of him.

"I'll wear it for the ceremony, Mum, but not now. Please!"

"Yes, now. You have to get used to the feel of it."

"It feels like a dress."

"Just do it!" called Megs from the sofa. She turned to the older girl for support. If Lucy thought he should try it on, it must be right!

His mum stifled his protests by whipping the costume down over his head and shoulders. "How does it feel now?" she asked.

"I don't honestly feel any different. Look, Mum, I'm not going through with this ceremony unless these three go with me." He pulled the costume over his head and handed it back to his mum.

"Of course they are going with you! They have all contributed in some way to restoring the necklace. They will walk at your side."

"What about Gregory?" asked Megs.

"Gregory will be the star of the show. Without him there wouldn't be a necklace."

Gregory rose slowly to his feet. "I shall do my best, despite my ageing limbs," he agreed, "to put on a creditable performance, as this may be my last show on this earth. But no encores, please! I'm too old for all that." He lowered his head and sank into a comfortable silence by the fireside.

There was a pause while they tried to work out what he'd said.

"Are we taking the green bus again?" asked Megs. "I liked that bit."

"We might as well," agreed Josh's stepdad. "The procession starts at the terminus."

"Good," said Josh. "Then Megs can stop off and see her friend, Sybil the sybil."

"She's gone," announced Josh's stepdad. "I went there yesterday. A new lady has taken her place.

"She must be somewhere!" said Josh. "Come on, Megs. That's worth two Esmeraldas."

Josh's stepdad laughed. "I don't know about that, Josh. Your mum usually gives you that information for free." He gave a passable imitation of his mum's voice. "Now come on, Josh. Where did you last see it? It must be somewhere."

"That's only because he keeps losing things," said his mum, appealing to the girls for support.

Sandy was stirring on the sofa. "Mr Flagsmith?"

"Yes, Sandy?"

"Did you ever find out what happened to the man calling himself Frederic Forbes?"

"Yes, Sandy. He's in prison, which is really the safest place for him with the Prince's men out looking for him."

"He seemed like a nice bloke. Why did he do it?"

Josh shuddered. An image crossed his mind of that gnome-like figure sitting in his attic room offering him crab and cucumber sandwiches. Was he responsible for the bomb which killed Frederic Forbes? No, that was the circlet. But he must have known about it!

"I think he was a collector," his stepdad replied. "His fascination for those stones got the better of him. That's why he stole the stone of knowledge. He hoped to gather all the stones for himself, but the Prince's offer was too good to refuse. And the Prince made it easy for him. All he had to do was steal the poisoned toad and pass it on to those two pirates that broke into the house. He swears – and I think he's telling the truth – that he had no idea what they were going to do with it."

"But he nearly killed Josh!" Lucy protested.

"Yes, Lucy," Josh's mum agreed. "And he would have succeeded had it not been for you and Megs, and your stone of course. But I agree with my husband."

"That's a first, at any rate!" exclaimed Josh's stepdad.

His mum ignored him. "If that man had any sense, he would have realised that the Prince always intended to kill him as soon as he got those stones. Much the easiest way – remove the evidence and avoid paying the ransom."

Josh's stepdad opened the door to let in Feathers and John Bosworthy. "Ah! Good! Just in time. I'll switch on the tele! Come on, you kids! Off the sofa. You'll have to make do with the carpet. We're all going to watch the Prince!"

"He's going to be interviewed," Josh's mum explained. "Here, Megs, here's your cushion." She put an arm on Lucy's shoulder. "She likes to throw cushions at the tele, don't you, Megs, when the interviewers annoy you?"

Megs grinned at Lucy in a shamefaced way and put the cushion aside.

"Don't worry, Megs," Josh's stepdad called out as he fiddled with the controls. "You won't need your cushion this time. The Maxtrader media chain is on our side!"

The four adults squeezed onto the sofa, with the two boys sprawled in front of them. Lucy brought chairs for herself and Megs and placed them alongside.

"Put on your necklace now, Josh," murmured his mum. "I have a feeling you may need it." Josh allowed his mum to come over and drape the ornate gold chain with its three onyx stones round his neck, feeling suddenly small and silly and intensely aware that everyone was watching him. He had lain awake dreading this moment. Could this necklace really cure his epilepsy - if not now, maybe later when he placed it in the temple?

"How do you feel?" asked Megs.

"I don't feel any different," he mumbled.

"You look different in that outfit," said Megs. "You remind me of Sybil the Sybil."

"Sh! Everyone," said his stepdad. "This thing is about to start."

The screen flickered into life. The camera focused on the reporter, standing outside a small, whitewashed bungalow in

Windfree.

"I've been there!" cried Josh. "That's the Prince's house!"

The reporter's face filled the screen now. He wore his sarcastic expression, the one he reserved for politicians. "We've just been treated–" he began, lingering on the word 'treated', "to a most dramatic piece of news. The man who likes to refer to himself as 'the Rebel Prince' claims to have found the Guardian's necklace. He is referring, of course to the three stones which were separated nearly four hundred years ago at the Treaty of the River Snake."

"Oh dear! Sorry, everyone!" exclaimed Josh's stepdad. "I had no idea he was going to come up with that one!"

"That's ridiculous!" shouted Megs. "The stones are sitting right here round Josh's neck!"

"Sh!"

"Anyway," she protested, "he doesn't want the necklace. He only wants to destroy it."

The scene switched to a shot of the Rebel Prince leaving the arena where he had just been addressing his cheering troops. He still wore his plain white robes, but this time adorned with an elegant golden necklace bearing three onyx pendants.

"So you say you found them, just like that?" asked the reporter in a tone of obvious disbelief, stumbling to keep up with him.

"No, no, Geoffrey, that's what you say, "replied the Prince mildly. "I think we had better get that right for the benefit of your viewers. The stone of love has always been in my possession. It is the stone I inherited from my famous ancestor. The other two stones I had the good fortune to acquire only recently."

"Acquire as in purchase or steal? I think it is reasonably well-known that one of these stones is in the possession of a boy called Josh Flagsmith."

"Hey!" cried Sandy, "You can tell he doesn't believe him."

"He believes what he's told to believe," explained John Bosworthy. "Magnus Maxtrader has decided that the Prince is bad for business."

"Let people think what they like," said the Prince pleasantly. "The rich and powerful of this world will support colonist oppression wherever they find it, but the true followers of mine, those that wish to return to the simple ways of the Rebel Prince, will know that these are the stones of the true Guardian and all other stones are fake."

Josh felt a surge of power run through him. He couldn't tell at first if this was just a surge of anger at having to sit and watch a man telling such a blatant lie. But automatically his hand went to the stones draped round his neck and he lovingly fingered each stone in turn. Then, in a way that he'd never experienced before, he felt the surge well up inside him and fill his chest with the power that Matilda must have felt four hundred years before.

"I can do this!" he shouted. "I can finish it all now!" The room had gone quiet now. He knew without looking round that all eyes were focussed on him. He looked up at the screen.

The Prince was back in the arena now. On either side of him, twelve armed guards stood at attention in their long white robes and concealed circlets, chests puffed out, eyes blazing with devotion or fear. He'd soon know how they really felt about their Prince!

The Prince held up the fake necklace for all to see. Josh could see the small onyx stone of truth dangling on one side and the stone of knowledge on the other and, in the centre just below them, he saw the fake stone of love, larger than the others.

Josh thought of all the dangers he and his friends had faced to obtain those stones, only to see their achievement snatched away by this mad playboy with the taunting smile. The anger gave him strength for what he needed to do. He fondled the true stone of love in his hand and focussed his new-found power on the fake stone that the Prince held out for his viewers to see.

Everyone in the room saw it. And heard it, too; as loud and clear as the cracking of a nut.

The stone split.

"Did you hear that?" asked Sandy.

"Of course we heard it!" shrieked Megs.

Then they heard two more cracks and, out of the cracked stones, a red liquid fell drop by drop onto the Prince's robes and onto his soft, white hands.

"The stones are bleeding!" cried Megs.

"He's got blood on his hands," said Feathers, "as if we didn't know."

Josh had to admire the way the Prince kept his cool. He looked down and smiled at the fake stones that had dropped from the necklace into his blood-stained hands with faked delight. Then he turned to the camera and said, "This is what I wanted everyone to see. The necklace of harmony is broken. There is no room for harmony on the western isles. Let pirates on every island arise and break their chains. The age of colonist oppression is over."

But suddenly, the screen went blank. A few seconds later, some adverts appeared, including the image of a girl washing her hands in Maxtrader soap. Then an announcer, sitting at her desk in the newsroom, apologised for the sudden break in transmission. There had just been a minor explosion which had put the line to Windfree out of action. Viewers would be glad to know that their reporter was safe. The Prince was currently unavailable for comment.

Josh's dad quickly switched off the telescreen. Josh sat on the carpet with hunched shoulders and listened to everyone praising him and talking about the power of his necklace. The adults stood in a group and discussed what it all meant and what would happen to the Prince and whether this meant his threat was finished. Sandy and Lucy and Megs seized the vacant sofa and talked about what they'd seen over and over again in giggles and whispers.

He didn't feel like joining in. He felt amazed and shaken by his experience and didn't want to talk about it. His mum came and sat beside him and put an arm round his shoulder and talked breathlessly about his special 'gift' and the magic of Matilda, but he felt too confused to take it all in. Then his stepdad patted him on the back and said 'Well done, my boy' and invited him to join him in the garden. "It's a bit quieter there," he explained.

"I just wanted to tell you that I'm very proud of you, Josh," he began, once they were sitting side by side on a garden bench in the shade of an overarching cedar. "Epilepsy itself is an amazing burden but look how you handled it!"

"What do you mean, Dad?"

"Well, I have no idea how the process works. But I wouldn't call it magic. The scientists in those days were vastly more experienced than our own. They created those stones as a cure for epilepsy and ended up with something infinitely more powerful. Anyway," he said, getting up and preparing to go inside, "You won't have to worry about these things much longer, "because, in a little while, these stones will be safely stowed in the temple and your epilepsy will be cured."

Josh looked at his watch. It felt peaceful, sitting out in the garden in the warmth of a summer evening. But he wondered if it was really that simple. He was still the Guardian, though he didn't know what use he would be without the Guardian's stones. Did that still make him a target? And the Prince hadn't really been defeated because he didn't need that necklace to win pirates to his cause. Those pirates from Northwoods would follow him to the ends of the earth so long as he promised to avenge their ancient wrongs.

He checked his watch again and went inside to join his friends. In an hour's time, his epilepsy would be cured. He felt a surge of joy, knowing that he was among his family and friends, and would soon be travelling up the mountain to surrender his stones in the Temple of Harmony.

The Neustrian Princess - Book 3 in The Island Wars

Chapter One

C ycling home from another great party in the centre of town, Josh kept his head down and pedalled hard along the wide, lighted avenue lined with orange trees and bougainvillea, his brain spinning with the sights and smells of this small, southern island. A warm, tropical breeze ruffled his hair as he headed out of town.

He rose in his seat to gain speed. Feathers would feel bound to wait up for him. That's what would annoy the old man most. Megs too. He pictured her black eyes smouldering with reproach. He should have 'left earlier' when some of his friends left. Megs had suddenly become the responsible one, though she was a good year younger than himself.

His legs ached as he pedalled up the steep gradient towards the dimly lit outskirts of town. He knew the old man worried about his safety - but he didn't feel afraid in Amaryllis. Being the Pirate Guardian made him a bit of a celebrity. He liked the way people recognised him on the streets and called out to him. Still, he felt bad about Feathers. He looked down at the road sliding back beneath his pedalling feet. Not much further to go. He had reached the top of the hill by the lighted monument and was freewheeling now along the dark stretch of road that curved downwards past the docks and up again towards the pink and white holiday bungalows that lined the coast.

He didn't have any lights on his bicycle. Nobody seemed to mind in Amaryllis, but he could barely see what lay in front of him. He put his head down and pedalled hard through this murky area of wasteland and dimly lit estates. He'd been stopped more than once by strangers stepping out in front of him, begging or threatening. He usually swerved past them, ignoring their jeers as he sped on out of sight. Tonight, he heard nothing – only the sound of raucous celebrations from the lighted centre of town behind him.

He heard the roar of a motorbike from the top of the hill by the monument. He'd noticed those motor bikes, revving their engines up and down outside the house where the party was being held. Another roar followed. Then they all started, like cocks competing for their kingdom.

He fixed his eyes on the kerb and the shadows of the docks beyond. The next street on his left was Mile End Road, the last and oldest street in town, a narrow, cobbled lane of small, terraced houses leading down to the docks. He always passed it in a hurry. It looked like the kind of street to avoid after dark.

The roar of the motorbikes had grown louder. They had almost caught up with him. He welcomed their company and slowed up a little, hugging the kerb to leave room for them to overtake. To his surprise, they slowed down too. They'd cut their engines and opted to fall in line behind him.

That didn't feel right. Bikers liked to laugh and josh one another. These guys just hung on his tail; a whole gang of them. He pedalled on, expecting them at any moment to roar past him. Instead, they slowed up. Their silence began to unnerve him. What were they waiting for? His eyes scanned the road for a possible escape route. The semi-darkness stretched ahead for about a mile. He pressed hard on the pedals.

Then a rough voice from the back of the group shouted, "Josh? That your name? Josh?" The unfriendly tone shot a wave of tension down his neck and shoulders. He tightened his grip on the handlebars. Another, younger, voice right behind him said, "Yea, that's him." He pedalled hard, eyes scanning the side of the road for a bolthole.

Suddenly, two bikes roared past, nearly knocking him off his bike as they brushed past him, pushing him into the kerb and swerving round to block him off. Others pressed him from behind, one of them bumping his back wheel. His heart beat furiously as he gripped his handlebars, hunting for a plan of escape.

A huge guy in a black leather jacket dismounted and loomed over him, blocking his escape. In a dreamlike trance of fear, Josh stared at the letters 'RR', picked out in white on the man's chest.

The man raised one hand to his mates, who laughed and went silent. He looked down at Josh. "Phone!" he said, holding out a hand to receive it.

Josh was in a place where he didn't want to be, late at night, in a deserted part of town. With sweaty hands, he fumbled for his phone. If this was a mugging, maybe they'd let him go. The man gave him a hard stare, took the phone and smashed it against the handlebars, tossing the pieces behind him. Josh gulped. He felt himself drowning in a sea of hostile faces.

The guy let go of his handlebars. "We're taking you down to the docks," he said, "for a little talk." The others laughed.

That did it. Josh slipped off his bike and ran.

Amid shouts and muffled curses, he stumbled over the grass verge and raced down the nearest side street. Behind him he heard sounds of a hasty conference; the big guy giving orders and the rest, who seemed to be younger, falling into line. His dash for freedom must have taken them by surprise, because he heard no immediate attempt to follow him. Then, as he raced down the dark, narrow street, he saw why they took their time. They'd forced him left off the avenue, down Mile End Road. Some of them were revving up their bikes and heading off – they'd sweep round to meet him at the docks!

He glanced round to see two shadows, including the heavy shape of the man he feared most, making their slow, purposeful descent. Sweating now, he raced down the dark, narrow street, desperate to put more space between himself and his pursuers.

He heard their heavy boots clattering on the cobbles behind him. They didn't sound in a hurry. They knew he had nowhere to go. As he ran, his eyes darted from side to side, searching for an alleyway that offered a means of escape. On either side, an unbroken line of dark, terraced houses stretched down towards that murky space where the street ended, and the rest of their gang would lie in wait. His two pursuers followed at a distance, like beaters driving him into a trap.

Panting, he saw a single lighted window halfway down the street; then another light on the other side; and another. He raced towards the lights. There must be hundreds of people crammed into those tiny houses, all asleep. An army of people! If only they could help him! Maybe, if he started ringing doorbells, somebody would let him in. He'd reached the lights by now and tried one door, then another. He looked round. His pursuers had made no effort to catch up. He listened for their footfalls and saw their dark shapes in the distance; just two of them, but bigger than him and probably armed with knives. Still, he stood a better chance against those two than facing the whole gang at the end of the street. Except one of them was that big guy with 'RR' on his chest! 'RR' – Rupert the Rebel. This was no ordinary biker.

He felt in his pockets for a weapon, but he didn't even have a penknife. Then he saw a few loose cobbles at the side of the street. Not much use against that guy, but it made him feel better holding one in each hand. He picked them up.

Then he had a better idea. He stopped and tossed one of the cobbles at a lighted window. He heard a tinkle of glass and saw a few scattered shards fall at his feet. They might not answer doors, these people, but surely a broken window would get some reaction! He looked up. No sound. Nothing. His pursuers saw what he was up to and quickened their pace. He put the other cobble in his right hand and aimed at the next house, but fumbled and missed.

The two bikers had broken into a run. He fumbled around for more stones and tried again. Another tinkle of glass. And the next. What was it with these people? He expected lights to go on and angry faces to peer out of their windows. His pursuers were hurrying now, but he knew he could outrun them if he tried. He gathered all the stones he could hold and flung them up at the windows on his own side of the street.

A light went on in the window opposite. A wave of hope washed over him. He waited with clenched fists for the window to open. Another light shone in the window next door and a voice called "Hoy!"

He felt a huge release of tension, hearing that angry voice shouting at him from the window where he'd thrown the first stone. "Hoy!" Then another window opened. The bikers stood in the shadows, watching. From the first house, a large bald man in a brown dressing gown stuck his head out of the window. "You've broken my window!" he shouted.

"He's broken mine too!" cried a shrill voice from the house next door.

"You just wait, young man," bellowed another voice from the house behind him. "I'm coming after you!"

Let him come soon!

"You've broken my window!" repeated the bald man in the dressing gown.

Josh stepped into the middle of the street in full view of the lighted window. For a moment, those men looked poised to make a dash from the shadows and grab him, but they hung back. He looked up at the windows. "I can explain!" he shouted.

"Hang on a minute, Ed!" cried the shrill voice. "I know that, young man. He's the Pirate Guardian."

"I don't care if he's the Pirate King, Nora!" cried the first voice. "He's broken my window."

"Pirates don't have kings," said the shrill voice. "They have princes, and they have Guardians. Besides, he says he can explain."

"Explain what? He's broken my window. Anyway, we don't have proper Guardians anymore; leastways not ones that go round breaking windows."

Josh gasped as a brawny arm tightened its hold round his windpipe. "The police will be here in a minute," said the man from the house behind him, giving his windpipe another squeeze. "You'll see."

"He's famous!" cried the shrill voice. "Lay off of him, Bill. You're choking him." More front doors opened, and their owners spilled out onto the street. Josh grinned as he saw his pursuers edging away from the scene. The grip on his throat relaxed, and he found himself surrounded. Some of the onlookers, mostly women, took the side of the shrill voice. "Let go of his neck," they cried. "He's only a lad! You're throttling him!" Others inclined to the male side of the argument; "He's broken my window!" roared the first voice, "and yours too," he added as an afterthought.

"He says he can explain," said the shrill voice.

"He can explain all he wants, and when he's finished, I'll hit him," said the man with the arm round Josh's neck.

"They tried to kill me," said Josh, seizing his chance to move the conversation along a bit.

"Who tried to kill you?"

"That's no excuse for breaking my window!"

"Hang on! I said who tried to kill him?"

"He could have knocked on my door."

"Pull the other one, Bill! When's the last time you ever opened the door to a stranger at night?"

"Well, I didn't see anyone trying to kill him."

"That's because you were asleep!"

Josh found himself surrounded by curious faces. "I wanted to wake you up so that you could save my life," he shouted. The crowd had stopped talking now, so he lowered his voice. "I'm sorry about the windows but I was being chased by a gang on motorbikes." Some of the onlookers cast doubtful stares up and down the street. "They chased me up the avenue," he said. "They had RR printed on their jackets – Rupert the Rebel. They left their motor bikes up there and followed me here on foot. The rest are waiting for me by the docks."

The crowd went silent. He felt the arm being released from his neck. "Bikers!" said the man, shaking the stiffness out of his arm. "You know what, lad? You've given me a cramp," he added, as if it was Josh's fault that he'd hurt his arm trying to strangle him. His neighbours waited. He was clearly a bit of a leader in that street. "Bikers!" he snorted. "We know that lot! Come on, young man. I think we'd better get you home."

"What about the police?" asked the shrill voice.

"I didn't call them, did I? What policeman would lose sleep over a broken window in Mile End Road?"

Josh heard murmurs of agreement. He found himself among friends. Bit by bit, as they accompanied him back to the avenue, they pieced together the story of the young Pirate Guardian being waylaid by a gang of bikers in the pay of the Rebel Prince. They found his bike where he'd left it, lying with its wheels up on the side of the avenue. They even insisted on walking him part of the way home until he reached the line of pink and white bungalows where he mounted his bicycle and pedalled off up the lighted avenue that led to his home. He laid his bike against the wall of the bungalow and shrugged off the events of the night. Next came the difficult bit. He tapped lightly on the front door.

Megs came to the door and held up a hand to caution him against going inside. "Sh! Feathers is asleep," she warned him.

"What time did he fall asleep?" whispered Josh.

"Ten o'clock."

She noticed his relief. Her face darkened. "Look, you're not getting away with this, Josh!"

"They tried to kill me."

"Seriously?"

"Yes, seriously! Bikers. One of them had 'RR' printed on his jacket. They probably all did, but I couldn't see in the dark."

Her eyes widened. She tugged his arm and said, "Come on. Let's go inside."

They sat opposite each other at the kitchen table.

"They smashed my phone and chased me down Mile End Road," Josh explained. He told her about the chase. She giggled when he got to the bit about the broken windows. But when he'd finished, she gave him a solemn look and shook her head. "What time did you leave the party?" She asked.

"I don't know. About twelve."

Megs gave a wry smile. "Come on, Josh," she said. "You know exactly. You're always looking at your watch. What time was it?"

He hesitated. "12h30," he admitted. "Why does it matter?"

"For goodness' sake, Josh! Your mum would go crazy if she knew. Why else did your parents send us to Amaryllis? It's meant to be safe for you here, but nowhere is completely safe at that time of night."

He shrugged. He didn't have an answer to that one.

She leaned back and smiled. "Tell me about the party," she said. "Were many people there?"

He knew where this question was leading. "Some of my year group," he said.

"Was Sharon there?" she asked

"Yea, some of the time."

"What's she like?"

"I don't know. All right."

"Did you kiss her?"

"Yea, sort of."

"Only sort of?" She gave a mischievous grin.

He remembered Sharon's kiss, her soft lips seeking his with sudden knowingness in the darkened room. He tried to shake the memory away.

"What are we going to do about those bikers?" Megs asked. "Tell your parents?"

"No way. They'd probably call us home or ask for a 24-hour guard on the house and Feathers would go mental. Can you imagine? We've got to work this one out by ourselves."

To his surprise, she nodded. "The Prince wants to kill you," she said finally. "We know that at least. He can't claim to rule the pirate world while people are still running around saying. Look, there's Josh! He's our Guardian!"

Josh felt as if he'd opened a door into a dark space. "What can I do? If the Prince is still out to get me, he has spies everywhere – even on Amaryllis. So I won't be safe until someone kills him, which doesn't look like happening."

Megs nodded and got up from the table. "Poor boy!" she said. "We'll think of something. Let's talk some more in the morning."

ABOUT THE AUTHOR

Donald, his wife Joey, and George, the very demanding collie.

Donald Frank Brown was born in Inverness, Scotland, in 1943 during the second world war. In his gap year, before studying English at Exeter College, Oxford, he worked in Paris selling the New York Times outside the Louvres. After teaching English in Brighton and the United Nations school in New York, he settled in Jersey and founded a language school. He is married with three children, ten grandchildren and one great grandchild.

Also by the Author

The House at the Edge of the World - The Island Wars Book 1

The Neustrian Princess - The Island Wars Book 3

Printed in Great Britain
by Amazon